ZANE PRESENTS

ALL ABOUT

Him

Dear Reader:

Meet Felicia Spears, the ultimate ride-or-die chick, standing by her man's side through the ups and downs of his singing career. She goes to all ends to satisfy and cater to Cooper—seeking steady gigs at local venues and promoting his talent.

Her singer husband eventually rises to the top, thanks to her ongoing efforts. But their relationship turns sour once he walks out. When he later marries his second wife, Evelyn, Felicia becomes enraged as she covets the new couple's lavish lifestyle, one that she feels she deserves. After all, she was the one who had sacrificed to ensure Cooper's success.

Her next mission is revenge. She's determined to reveal a darker side of the now popular artist. It's an image that isn't reflected in his lyrics.

Pat has the knack for telling stories that often are straight from the headlines. Her novels *Daddy by Default* and *Party Girl* focus on legal issues surrounding paternity and Texas laws. Her *Guarding Secrets* exposes corruption within the walls of a correctional facility.

As always, thanks for supporting myself and the Strebor Books family. We strive to bring you the most cutting-edge, out-of-the-box material on the market. You can find me on Facebook @AuthorZane.

Zane

Publisher
Strebor Books
www.simonandschuster.com

ZANE PRESENTS

ALL ABOUT

Him

PAT TUCKER

SBI

STREBOR BOOKS

NEW YORK LONDON TORONTO SYDNEY

Strebor Books
P.O. 55471
Atlanta, GA 30308
www.simonandschuster.com

ISBN 978-1-59309-684-7
ISBN 978-1-50111-955-2 (ebook)
LCCN 2017941825

First Strebor Books trade paperback edition November 2016

Cover design: www.mariondesigns.com
Cover photograph: © Keith Saunders/Keith Saunders Photos

10 9 8 7 6 5 4 3 2 1

Manufactured in the United States of America

For information regarding special discounts for bulk purchases, please contact Simon & Schuster Special Sales at 1-866-506-1949

The Simon & Schuster Speakers Bureau can bring authors to your live event. For more information or to book an event, contact the Simon & Schuster Speakers Bureau at 1-866-248-3049 or visit our website at www.simonspeakers.com.

Acknowledgments

I remain honored to be able to once again, give gratitude for all of the blessings bestowed upon me. I thank God for his continued favor... As always, unlimited appreciation goes to my patient and wonderful mother, Deborah Tucker Bodden; my lifelong cheerleader, and the very best sister a girl could have, Denise Braxton; my patient and loving husband, Coach Wilson, thanks for your love, and support. I'm a handful, but Coach is in it for the long haul and he understands: the good stuff never goes on sale! I'd like to thank my handsome younger brother, Irvin Kelvin Seguro and Amber; the two best uncles in the world, Robert and Vaughn Belzonie...

Aunts, Regina, and Shelia..., my loving and supportive family in Belize, Aunt Elaine, Therese, my cousins, Patrick, Marsha, and Cassandra, and the rest of my cousins, nephews, nieces, and my entire supportive family including my older brother, Carlton Anthony Tucker, who hustles to sell my books to anyone who will listen and buy a copy! If you know me well, you know I'm a walking poster girl for my beloved Sorority, Sigma Gamma Rho Sorority, Inc., but my love goes even deeper for my Sorors, Miranda Moore, Nikki Brock, Karen Williams, Jeness Sherell, Gloria Shannon, Keywanne Hawkins, Desiree Clement, Yolanda Jones, and the rest of those exquisite ladies of Sigma Gamma Rho Sorority Inc. and especially all of my sisters of the Glamorous Gamma Phi Sigma Chapter here in Houston, TX. I'm blessed to be surrounded by friends who accept me just the way I am. ReShonda Tate Billingsley—Thanks for your constant support, listening ear, and unwavering faith in my work. Victoria Christopher Murray, your kindness, giving heart, and willingness to help others are the truth! Special thanks to my agent, Sara, and a world of gratitude to my Strebor family, the dynamic duo Zane, and Charmaine, for having faith in my work. Special thanks to the publicity Queens led by Yona Deshommes at Strebor who help spread the word about my work.

Again, I saved the very best for last, _____ (your name goes there!) Yes, you, the reader! I'm so honored to have your support—I know you are overwhelmed by choices, and that's what makes your selection of my work such a humbling experience. I will never take your support for granted. There were so many bookclubs that picked up Daddy by Default, Football Widows, Party Girl, Daddy's Maybe, and A Social Affair, I wanted to honor some of you with a special shout-out: The bible of AFAM Lit: Johnnie Mosely and the rest of the wonderful men who make up Memphis' Renaissance Men's book club, Sisters are Reading Too (They have been with me from day 1!!)

Special thanks to Divas Read2-Happy Hour-Cush City-Girl-friends, Inc.-Drama Queens-Mugna Suma-First Wives-Brand Nu Day-Go On Girl, TX 1-As the Page turns-APOO, Urban Reviews, OOSA, Mahogany Expressions, Black Diamonds, BragAbout Books, Spirit of Sisterhood, and so many more, I appreciate you all! If I forgot anyone, and I'm sure I have, always, charge it to my head and not my heart. As always, please drop me a line at rekcutp@hotmail.com or sylkkep@yahoo.com I'd love to hear from you, and I answer all emails. Connect with me on Facebook, and follow me on Twitter @authorpattucker-I follow back! And I love taking pics…mostly selfies, so check me out on IG as well.

"Everybody knows God gives extra blessings to those who date the ugly. I mean, c'mon, Felicia."

My BFF's tone was as stiff as an upper lip as she tried to convince me that I needed to get with a guy from my night job. Yesterday, Jones' logic was that another man, even one who needed a brown paper bag over his head in public, would help me bounce back and forget about my painful divorce.

Forget the fact that the man was not attractive in any way; the fact that he was a willing man, should have been enough for me. I was trying to be low-key. I listened, but I wasn't really feeling her or her logic.

"Besides, when we close our eyes, everyone can look like Dwayne Johnson, or Denzel," she said, as she turned the car onto my street. She had a point there, but not enough for me to get with a man whose face I couldn't stomach. Although Yesterday and I had been friends for most of our thirty-six years on this earth, we rarely agreed on anything.

She was the only person I could call when I needed a ride back from the airport after my disastrous trip to Los Angeles. But even what I found in that hotel room couldn't prepare me for what my eyes took in.

I looked around, and before I could process her *advice*, I struggled with what I saw. Suddenly, panic attacked my entire nervous system with incredible strength. Yesterday hadn't even brought the car to a complete stop, but I snatched the door open and jumped out. My heart plummeted to the bottom of my feet.

"What the hell?!" Yesterday screeched, once she got out of the car and tried to catch up with me.

But I was already gone. What I saw literally took my trapped breath away and left me hyperventilating.

Shoes, clothes, old ratty lingerie, everything I owned was sprawled across the grass. Everything, including the old wooden jewelry armoire that belonged to my late grandmother, had been thrown out.

My head started to swim and my heart was nearly off the chart. I couldn't find the words or the strength. To my right, from the corner of my eye, a man rummaged through a pile of my clothes.

"Hey! That's mine!" I yelled at the homeless man who seemed so startled by the sound of my voice, he dropped the bag he had and quickly scurried away.

My head felt light as I looked around and tried to take inventory, but it was hard. My eyes wouldn't stop watering. I swallowed hard and dry, like a dusty cactus had lodged itself down my throat. How long had my things been outside for any and everybody to pick over? Why the hell would Cooper toss my stuff out like everyday trash?

Yesterday was nearly out of breath when she walked up to me, and then she stopped and looked around.

"Uh, why is all your shit out here like this?"

She looked around the space and took in the same heart-wrenching sight that nearly caused me to fall out.

"I swear, I hate men!"

Yesterday sprang into action. She grabbed a bag and started to stuff it with clothes, shoes, and toiletries.

Unable to move, I stood there under Houston's relentless sun, as warm tears ran down my cheeks.

How had my life crumbled so quickly?

Tears might have been falling, but I was more pissed, than hurt. I wanted revenge, and the fact that I didn't know how I could possibly get it had literally reduced me to a messy puddle of tears. It wasn't fair that he was still on top.

"You need to come on," Yesterday said as she put down a full bag and picked up an empty one.

The reality of my situation prevented me from moving. I was homeless and would need to completely start over.

When the golf cart pulled up next to us, Yesterday stopped and huffed in my direction. But the man behind the wheel caught our full attention.

"You got an hour, Ma'am. We're gonna need you to clear your belongings off the property or else we're gonna need to call maintenance to dispose of it," the uniformed security officer said.

"What the hell do you think we're doing?!" Yesterday yelled. She threw enough attitude to him for both of us. I was spent, and couldn't muster up any energy.

"There's no way I can move all of this stuff in an hour," I hollered at him.

"Let's try," Yesterday said.

"You have one hour. Whatever you don't take will be disposed of," the guard said.

There was no sensitivity in his voice, and that made me wonder whether he considered Cooper a friend. Yesterday worked to stuff a third bag. My things were everywhere. How could this have happened to me?

"Where's the rest of my stuff?" I looked around. Everything that was scattered belonged to me and only me. I wondered about the sofa, the breakfast table, the bedroom suite. Had someone already come by and picked through what they wanted?

Houston was always hot and humid, but on this day, it felt unbearable. Perspiration rolled down my back, my armpits, and the sides of my head. But I couldn't be sure whether the heat I felt was from the sun or from the realization that I had lost complete control. My life was barely recognizable, and it scared the shit out of me.

I turned to the security guard. "Where's the rest of my things? My furniture?"

He shrugged, then pulled a radio from his golf cart. He drove up a few feet away from us and pressed a button. I couldn't make out what he said, but he spoke into the radio, then pulled it up to his ear.

A few minutes later, he put the cart in reverse. The beeping noise worked what was left of my frayed nerves. I hadn't moved from the spot he'd left me in.

"Manager says the guy took what he wanted and left the rest." He looked around at my life as it was sprawled across the grass. "Looks like he didn't want your stuff."

That made it hurt even more. Cooper never told me we needed to move. We'd stopped talking months ago when it became painfully clear that he was Team Evelyn. I always hoped things would somehow get better between us, but the wedge was hard to overcome. However, I remained optimistic for a long time.

Yesterday was on her fourth trip from the car to the lawn.

Suddenly, a man rode up on a bike, hopped off, looked at her, then looked at me.

"Felicia Spears?" he asked. But the way he looked between us, made it clear he wasn't sure who was whom.

"Yeah, who are you?" I eyed him suspiciously.

Before I could answer, he shoved a large envelope toward my chest and yelled, "You've been served." He hopped back on his bike and pedaled away faster than I'd ever seen any human move.

I didn't need to open it to know that Cooper had served me child custody papers. He was lower than the lowest life form.

"Look, you knew it was coming," Yesterday said. She huffed, looked around, then went back to work.

Although I knew it was coming, it didn't make it any easier to accept. I thought the business trip would help Cooper cool off, not give him time to get his ducks lined up and decide to divorce me and announce plans to fight me for full custody of our son.

The guard looked at me with pity in his eyes, and that made me feel worse.

"Listen, I gotta make my rounds. If I cover the entire complex, it's usually right at about two hours. You think that'll be enough time to clear the bulk of this stuff out?"

Warm embarrassment washed over me as I mustered up the strength to nod. I gladly accepted that olive branch he'd offered.

"A'ight then."

He threw his golf cart into gear and drove off. I was disgusted, but more than that, I was ashamed. Cooper had left me, taken our things, and had me served with court papers on the same day he knew I'd come home to find what was left of our life. That was heartless. But I knew that he hadn't acted alone, I knew who had put him up to this, and there was little I could do about it.

People gawked as they walked by, and that made everything one thousand times worse.

Yesterday suddenly stopped what she was doing and threw her hands to her hips.

"Look, it's too hot for me to be doing all of this by myself. You need to wipe your tears and help me pack up what you want."

She was right. I was grateful she was there to take charge of everything. I was a useless mess on two legs.

Cooper didn't even have the decency to face me. He took the

coward's way out even though I wouldn't have had too many words for him. He was in beautiful, sunny L.A., while my life was crumbling here in Houston.

"Stop feeling sorry for yourself and c'mon!" Yesterday yelled. I understood her growing frustration, but there was little I could do to fix it.

"C'mon!" Yesterday repeated.

I pulled in a deep breath and reached for a pillowcase. As I walked around the lawn near the front door of our former apartment, I still couldn't believe that this was my life.

He had won again!

Chapter One

"I wanna shoot him, I mean, kill his simple ass dead! I'm almost positive no jury would ever convict after they heard my story."

Yesterday's head whipped in my direction, and her eyes grew wide. She sighed and looked at me with pity in her eyes. It was an expression I had gotten used to over the past few years.

Five years ago, my worthless husband went on a business trip that was really a cover for the fact that he had left me. Soon thereafter, he became an overnight singing sensation, but not before my blood sweat and tears set the foundation for his success. I was certain he'd have a different version, but mine was closest to the truth, because the truth wasn't in him. Others might have forgotten, but I would always remember.

You know I'll have to testify to what I just heard you say, if I'm ever subpoenaed, right?" Yesterday joked. Her arched brow went up before she quickly jumped up from her seat and immediately fell under his spell. "Besides, if you killed Coop, millions of women would be devastated."

She clutched toward her chest as if she needed to emphasize her statement.

My stomach began to do that flip-flop thing that made me want to vomit.

Life wasn't fair. That was for sure, but how much bad luck did any one woman deserve? I'd had my share and then some.

"Girrrrrl, I still can't believe we know a bona-fide star," Yesterday said.

Her voice was laced with admiration and wonder. It was like she had no memory of the living hell that her so-called bona-fide star had put me through. My life had crumbled into millions of pieces, and all these years later, I still struggled to pay bills.

The fact that Yesterday continued to support his work, even a bootleg copy, felt like an epic betrayal. But considering how many so-called friends and relatives I had lost after he'd left me, there wasn't much I could do about her treachery. If I alienated her, I'd be alone.

Yesterday was up swaying to the music, her eyes closed and her hips gyrating like she was lost in a wonderful memory. I was disgusted every time I heard his voice blare through the speakers. In my car, I could change the station, but in a restaurant, there was nothing I could do. I was held hostage for the four-minute duration of his songs.

The sound of his voice crooning, singing all the things any woman would want to hear sickened me. I knew for certain that Cooper only loved himself. Despite the lyrics, I knew the truth. He probably didn't even write those words; Lord knew he didn't know what they meant.

"Oooh," snap, snap, "this is my jam." Yesterday's hips synchronized with the snaps of her fingers as she moved to the music.

"Ohmygod, I love this song," a woman said as she passed our table.

Yesterday's mood seemed to be broken long enough for her to point at me and say, "That's Coop, her ex-husband."

The woman's eyes nearly popped from their sockets. She doubled back and stood in front of our table.

"For real?" She was too giddy. "I knew that was him. I love his music." She turned to me. "You was married to Cooper Spears?"

Reluctantly, I nodded, despite that the way she asked told me she didn't believe it. Her eyes challenged my appearance. She probably wondered how someone who looked like me could've been married to such a handsome crooner who had all the right words.

Having not missed a beat, Yesterday fell back into her groove and picked up where she'd left off.

I wanted to snatch her back down onto her chair and tell her the damn song wasn't all that good. Yesterday was doing too much, but if I had said anything, it would have encouraged her to keep up the theatrics. I rolled my eyes and pulled the menu up to try and block her and all of the attention she brought to our table.

The waiter couldn't come fast enough. Sometimes I wondered whether Yesterday did all the extras as a way to pour salt on my wound, which she knew was still raw. It was hard, but I ignored her and her antics.

When the song finally went off, she flopped down into her seat and sighed real hard like it was all she could do to catch her breath. It didn't take all of that.

"Girl, I swear I love that song. Coop know good and well he did *that* with that song."

Chili's menu had never been so interesting. Did she really think I wanted to sit and talk about my ex and his latest hit song? She knew how long it took for me to get over what he had done to me, and it still hurt like hell.

"What you getting? I'm starving."

It must've been all the damn dancing. I suppressed another eye-roll, but finally, I calmed enough to move the menu and face her. Yesterday's eyes were glued to the menu as if she needed to focus on her options.

My appetite was nearly gone, but I needed to eat. Later, when I sat inside my tiny, one-room apartment alone, I'd be ready to kick myself over the hunger pangs.

Before I could say anything to Yesterday, a thin, plain woman with stringy hair slid in front of our table.

"So, who's Coop's ex-wife?" She looked back and forth between Yesterday and me. Excitement was all over her face.

Yesterday's finger flew up, and like the barrel of a gun, pointed directly at me.

"Wow! You were married to Coop? He's like one of my most favorite singers."

Again, the wonder in her voice told me she, too, was a nonbeliever.

My eyes danced around the restaurant as I searched for her manager. I didn't know whom I wanted to slap first—her or Yesterday—for being so nonchalant and telling the world my personal business.

"That's nice," I said dryly.

I glanced back down at the menu and hoped she'd take the hint. When I didn't say anything else about Coop, she pulled a tiny note-pad from her apron and pulled the pen from the side of her head.

"Do you ladies know what you're having?"

"I do. I'm so hungry I could eat two of these rib platters," Yesterday said.

"So, you want the ribs, a full or half order?"

"Umm, let me have the full order," Yesterday said.

Yesterday ordered her sides, and a drink, then looked at me. I placed my order and waited for the waitress to turn and leave.

Once she was out of earshot, I said to Yesterday, "Can you please stop telling people that Coop is my ex-husband?"

She leaned over the table.

Now she wanted to be discreet?

"Girl, why you mad?"

I studied her face.

"No, like seriously. Why you mad? Why not tell the world you his ex? So he's living his new fancy life with the new wifey by his side, and you down here looking in from the outside. Girl, you know that's supposed to be you up there on those award shows and on the red carpet with him." Yesterday sucked her teeth like the scenario really bothered her.

It was hard to ignore her because she'd keep going, but I didn't need to be reminded that Coop and his new wife were living *the* life while I just barely lived.

All I could think as Yesterday rambled on about a magazine spread she had seen, was that there had to be something better around the corner for me. Why would God allow me to live in a real-life hell right here on earth?

"...I'm serious. If I was you, everywhere I went, everybody would know I helped that nucca get to where he is today. Then when he got his big break, he dumped me after all I had done for him. You better than me, because I'd make sure anyone who would listen would hear my side of the story."

Yesterday worked my very last nerve. I hated Cooper for what he had done to me, but if I thought talking about it would in any way tarnish this new fancy life he had going, I probably would discuss it from sunup until no one else wanted to listen. But I knew it wouldn't. Or so I thought.

"You know those tabloid shows pay like thousands for dirt on celebrities."

"Nobody wants to hear about Cooper's tired self," I said.

Yesterday sucked her teeth.

"You need to get with it. Coop is haute right now. You kid yourself thinking nobody would want to hear some of his dirt. Umph. I know better!"

Was it possible that for once Yesterday knew what she was talking about? I didn't want to spend lots of time or energy thinking about him or even what others may have thought about him.

"Felicia, you know he's nominated for like three Grammys, right?"

Three? I thought I'd heard something about a nomination, but honestly, when anything about him came on TV or even the radio, that was a sign for me to find something else to do.

Who in the hell would pay thousands for dirt on my worthless ex-husband? As quickly as curiosity crept into my mind, I shook the thoughts away.

When my cell phone rang, I glanced down at the screen and cringed at the 866 number that I knew for certain was a bill collector's.

I was eating out only because Yesterday had agreed to treat to get me out of the apartment. Between the bills, and my overdrawn bank account, I needed to do something—and fast.

Chapter Two

The TV was usually on when I got ready for work, and today was no exception. But on this morning, when I turned on the local Fox station, what I saw made my knees nearly give way; I had to grab the wall to balance myself.

A roll of perspiration traveled from the nape of my neck down the middle of my back.

The newspeople were going on about Cooper and his Grammy nominations. In addition, they were talking about a local concert he was having at the Arena theater with Joe and Ginuwine.

I rolled my eyes hard.

When had *he* become that big? I used to like Ginuwine and Joe. Why in the world would they be doing a concert with Coop? I was baffled, but the real stunner came when they cut to a reporter who was out in the field.

My hope was that they'd move on to a different topic. Hadn't someone died during a robbery or a drag race? Where was the real news when we needed it? Why was Cooper receiving so much coverage?

"Yes, Jose, we are about to go inside Coop's swanky University Place house, where he and his wife make what they call 'magical music' together. We're told they often get inspiration right behind these doors."

The large wooden doors were fancy beyond belief. I wondered how much they cost.

The reporter walked up to the Spanish-inspired home that sat on a large piece of land with a dramatic fountain and gazebo in the circular cobblestone driveway.

My head started to spin.

The reporter rang the doorbell, and a loud, mystical-sounding chime rang out. A few seconds later, the door swung open, and Evelyn's gummy smile filled the camera lens. Time had done nothing to help minimize the hatred I felt for her. It was still real and very raw. If I could have gotten away with it, I would have killed her and not felt an ounce of guilt. As a matter of fact, it might have been worth the case I'd catch if I got caught.

"Good morning, we've been expecting you," she said and flashed another fake grin. She was ugly.

Cooper had left me for that mud-dog. But what bothered me more than the sheer hatred I felt for Evelyn, whom knew he was married when she'd moved in on him, was the fortress that the happy couple now called home.

The reporter walked into a brightly lit foyer. Just above her head, a crystal chandelier hung, and rows of skylights could be seen for miles ahead.

"This house is absolutely gorgeous," the reporter said as she looked around in wonderment.

Evelyn used her arm to make a sweeping motion. "We are truly blessed."

I wanted to vomit.

How could Coop afford such luxury? Was I really that disconnected from reality? When had he become a star of this magnitude?

My phone rang. I started to ignore it because I was completely enthralled by the tour of Coop's house. The phone stopped ringing just as I reached for it.

That allowed my focus to return to the TV. I watched as they walked down a hallway with the walls adorned with pictures of Coop, Evelyn, and *my* son. Their photos alluded to a life of sunshine, smiles, and riches.

As if the cameraman could read my thoughts, he tilted across the rows of family pictures. There were images on beaches, in Atlantic City, and even one with what looked like the Eiffel Tower in the background. There were times I could barely afford food, and they were living large?

My life had been snatched from me before I could live it.

When my phone rang again, I couldn't pull my eyes away from the TV screen, but I answered anyway.

"OHMYGOD! Felicia! Are you watching Fox? Guuurrrl, they are inside Coop's house! Jesus! I didn't know he had it like that! C'mon, please, you gotta turn it on; put your TV on Channel 26, girl! Now!"

Yesterday sounded possessed. Her voice was loud and bursting with excitement. She sounded like she might have had an aneurysm.

I held the phone, my eyes glued to the screen as Yesterday screamed in my ear. Her bubbly excitement was nearly too much for me to handle.

"This is one of our favorite rooms in the entire house," Evelyn boasted on the TV screen.

The camera did a quick pan of the vast room, then focused back on the two women. The reporter ooohed and aaahed at every turn.

Despite the envy I felt eating away at my heart, there was no denying, the room was breathtaking. The décor was done in cream with cherrywood panels that outlined mini-balconies on the upper level. The open space made the room appear larger than it probably was, but it worked. It looked comfy and inviting.

"Girl, you see that?" Yesterday asked.

I felt sick as the reporter went on and on about the custom tiles and the wood used for the panels.

"Look, Yesterday, I need to go; that's my other line," I lied.

"Okay, but you gotta call me back, so we can talk about this later."

Why would I want to talk any more about Coop's house, his new life, and everything else that I clearly did not have? I just needed to get off the phone with Yesterday; she didn't get it.

She didn't get that this was supposed to be *my* life with Cooper. When we were together, he didn't have a dime to his name; all he had was a dream. Before we'd moved into the apartment, we'd stayed with my mother. I'd had the vision for our future. I was the machine behind his powerful voice, and I'd laid the groundwork for his current success. There were times when I had to convince him that success was within reach, and it really was attainable.

But no one ever wanted to hear about that. Now that his star was shining brightly, people only remembered their encounters with him. They didn't remember what it had taken to get him where he was today.

Although I ended the call with Yesterday, I didn't put the phone down. I watched, seething with envy as the reporter followed Evelyn out to one of the most incredible outdoor kitchens I had ever seen. Their backyard was massive, with a waterfall, a pool, and a Jacuzzi.

I dialed the number to my day job at the processing center, where we handled orders from Amazon.com.

"Hi, this is Felicia. I can't come in today. I don't feel so hot."

My supervisor was cool; never asked too many questions. She told me to take as much time as I needed and feel better soon. My illness might not have been physical, but I felt awful.

Watching them show off Coop's incredible new house had literally made me sick.

Chapter Three

B eing home during a workday was like a form of torture. Daytime TV sucked. I watched the morning talk shows after the news went off, but I kept expecting *The View* to announce Cooper as their next guest. So, I couldn't focus. Someone had gone and flipped my world upside down by making all of his dreams, the very ones I'd planted, come true.

How had I missed out on his sudden rise to the top? I'd checked out for a while after he'd left me destitute, but I didn't think I had missed that much. This was such a sick joke; it had to be.

Tired of TV and unable to call anyone, because most people are at work during the day and can't talk on the phone, I stretched out on the sofa. My mind wouldn't allow me to sleep; it raced with thoughts of my early days with Cooper. We were newly married, still young and in love with unrealistic thoughts of what the future might hold.

"Baby, you got more talent in your pinky fingernail than Usher. You will get your shot."

Cooper's light eyes had locked on mine, but I could tell he didn't believe the words that had come out of my mouth. I believed in him and his talents. I wanted to build him up and let him know that I believed in his potential, despite where we were currently. We were young; we had lots of time.

"That's bullshit, Licia. You been saying that for two years now, and here we are, still sleeping in your mama's damn garage."

Coop turned his massive back to me, and I felt like a mound of warm shit. He was right; I had been making promises from the day I had decided to manage his career. Who knew music management would be this hard?

I started to rub his shoulders. My touch was light and feathery because I couldn't be sure how upset he was, and I didn't want him to explode. He was capable of the unexpected with no warning.

"The mayor's office didn't say no, but we need to be patient. I know you're tired of being at Milan's, but for now, that's our only paying gig, Babe, so I need you to be patient. Can you do that for me?"

By then I had gone from soft touches to strong kneading in his shoulder blades.

When I heard the deep groans escape his lips, I knew I was making progress. I just needed his mind to cooperate.

"Ain't this the second year you tried with the city?" Coop asked.

"Yeah, but I gotta keep asking. I can't quit just because I got a no."

Success took more than talent, and Coop didn't understand that. He felt like his talent and good looks should be more than enough to propel him to superstar status. He thought he was the only good-looking man with a great singing voice.

I eased my hands up to his neck and applied a little more pressure.

"Licia, I'm getting tired of this shit. After that fight broke out last weekend, it's hard to believe you booked me there again."

Everything Coop said was true. I shouldn't have agreed to come back to the club, but the truth was, if we dropped that weekly club gig, we'd be worse off than he could imagine. Once the original agreement expired, and I had nothing better, I jumped at the chance to renew.

"Baby, I sent them a list of demands and told them I wasn't putting up with any of that drunken bullshit."

He swung his head in my direction.

"You told them that?" Pleasure made its way to his features.

"Yeah. Listen, they need to treat you like the talent you are. Also, I gave them your rider too. I told Lenny that they need to have a green room set up for you by four on Friday. I gave him a list of all the items that need to be in that room, including the music that keeps you calm and demanded that he sign an agreement saying he understood and would abide by it."

Coop turned onto his back and looked me in my eyes.

"You said all that?"

I nodded.

He was completely engaged, and quite happy.

"What did Lenny say? Hell, what did Al say?"

"Well, Big Al is cool, but Lenny tried to say you're not personable, says you look down your nose at his staff and act like you're bigger than what you are." All of which was completely true.

Frown lines invaded Coop's forehead as he listened.

His head tilted ever so slightly. "He said that shit about me?"

His breathing started to escalate. I was trying to calm him, not stir shit up again.

"Baby, I got him good. But you know, I let him set the rope to hang himself. So he's going on talking about how it would help if you worked the room a little before your set."

Coop sighed hard. He shook his head as I continued.

"I told him, we're gonna need that green room, and we're gonna need the staff to understand you're not there to socialize. I explained that your voice is an instrument that requires the proper prep before each show, and if there's lots of chaos and antics going on, you can't perform to your full potential."

By now, Coop was up on his elbows and fully engaged in the conversation.

"That's what's up! Shiiiid, you think they mess with Prince or MJ before they hit the stage?"

"No, baby. They wouldn't dare."

There was no need for me to point out that Cooper couldn't read music, couldn't play any instruments, and he had not been performing since early childhood.

Instead, I allowed him to include himself in a circle that was years and works beyond his league or his potential.

"Yo, look, I'm just glad you finally started making some demands. You know how many people tell me the only reason they come there is because they know I'll be performing?"

He didn't give me a chance to determine whether it was a rhetorical question before he quickly answered.

"A lot. Hell, when I'm in Kroger, people are constantly stopping me to say they enjoyed the show, or they came just to see me." He paused for a moment. "I really think I've done a lot to increase traffic in that dump. They oughta be kissing the ground I step across."

My husband knew no boundaries. There was nobody who loved Cooper more than Cooper. He would brag about himself all day and night if he wasn't stopped.

Before I could regroup, Cooper moved in and his lips covered mine.

Nothing I said was meant to be an aphrodisiac, but it was clear Coop was feeling it. He rubbed my back and pulled me closer. The kiss was hot and hungry. As my eyes closed, and I lost myself in the ecstasy, I thought about how long it had been since we were intimate.

My husband was like no other. All that talk about his career and what I was going to do to make him shine was what did it for him.

He pulled my body close and all but ripped my clothes off. The lace-cup bra was pulled up without being unhooked, and he attacked my nipples like a man who hadn't eaten in days.

Everything felt good. I breathed hard and hot into his ear and licked his lobes.

Cooper fumbled between his legs and freed himself. I straddled him and sank down onto his stiff erection.

For a second, the expansion of him filled me and took my breath away. He felt good. I had forgotten what it felt like to make love to my husband. So much of what we talked about centered on his career and how I wasn't doing enough to make him a star.

"Damn," he moaned.

I clutched his neck and pulled him in closer. He manhandled my breasts and nearly drove me over the edge. I ground my hips into his lap and rode him unmercifully.

"Damn, Licia! Damn!"

The moment he exploded, I really felt like I had done my part to make him feel better. My pussy was still wet, throbbing, and hungry, but there was no way I could say that to Cooper. The truth was, when it came to sex, knowing he hadn't satisfied me would devastate him.

Once I rolled off of him, Cooper jumped up and rushed toward the bathroom. He slammed the door shut behind him, and I caught my breath.

A few minutes later, Cooper walked back into the room. I was a little pissed that he didn't think to bring me a towel.

Freshly showered, my husband's olive skin, short dark curly hair, and broad shoulders all made him look star-worthy. I knew the power of his intense eyes, so dreamy that looking into them too intently could literally get your juices flowing.

"So, did you ever hear back from the Wine Divas?"

I felt my heart beating in my ear. I was supposed to follow up on that last week and totally had forgotten. There was no way I could tell Coop that I had dropped the ball.

"Babe, I keep calling those people and still no response. I'm gonna make something happen, even if I have to go there myself."

His expression told me he didn't believe me.

"Don't be bullshitting me, Licia. You know I don't need all that extra shit you give to everyone else."

"No bullshit, but, baby, I need you to understand this all takes time. There's no other way for me to put it." I eased up and moved in on him.

"I'm gonna make you a star, babe, if it's the last thing I do."

Coop looked down at me.

"Licia, I'm already a star, baby. It's your job to make sure the rest of the world figures that out before it's too damn late! Ya feel me?"

I nodded.

"And if you can't do it, I need to find somebody who can."

He grabbed a T-shirt, and then walked out of the room. His aftershave lingered long after he was gone, and so did his threat.

Chapter Four

Laughter pulled me back from thoughts of the early days with Cooper. But it was the kind of laugh that happened when I really wanted to cry. My emotions had a way of taking over when I lost all control. This was usually the time when good thoughts escaped me, and I didn't know how to get back to being myself. I changed my clothes and fought the other urge. There was no way I should've been thinking about things that contributed to my self-destruction, but I could only fight for so long. The battle was an ongoing one, and it never seemed to let up.

Images of that fancy house flashed through my mind. I was weak. I needed something to help make me feel better.

I grabbed the remote and turned the TV off. I needed to be strong. Thoughts of Cooper's new life were enough to make me suicidal. I squeezed my eyes shut and settled back down onto the sofa.

There was nothing I could do to stop the images that seemed stuck on replay in my head. The curb appeal, the pristine foyer, the furniture that looked like it belonged in a model home; all of it was too much for me to handle. Two hours later, I rose from the sofa, yawned, stretched long and hard, and rubbed my eyes. It was still hard to fathom that Coop was living like a king. He didn't deserve the favor he had been shown; he really was a selfish narcissist.

The clock on the microwave flashed 5:18. My entire day had gone by in a flash. I bolted up, swung my legs over to the floor, and walked over to the small dresser. After much thought, I pulled out the fourth drawer.

"Shit, where is it?"

My nerves were bad.

After going through the entire drawer, I remembered that I had already used what was in there. What the hell would I do now? I eased up against the wall and slid down to the floor. My life was miserable. The tears pushed their way through before I could muster up the strength to try and stop them.

How had shit fallen apart for me but rose to the skies for him? Depression hovered over me like a full rain cloud ready to dump at any moment. I needed something to make this all go away, even if only temporarily.

Suddenly, I remembered my emergency stash. Excitement washed over me as I rushed to the kitchen, pulled open the pantry door, and grabbed the small pill box. It was hidden behind the Saltine crackers, for the most desperate of times. This had definitely met that criteria. I opened the small refrigerator and grabbed a bottle of wine.

Once I poured a glass full, I grabbed a pill, opened my mouth, tossed it to the back of my throat, and took a gulp of wine.

With my eyes squeezed shut, I took another healthy gulp of wine, allowed my jaws to expand to hold more liquid, and prayed that the mixture would work with lightning speed.

I needed to go to another place, and I needed to go there as quickly as possible.

In my mind, I warned myself that another pill so soon wouldn't be the best thing to do. But my heart said something else. What was the worst that could happen, considering I was living one step from homelessness while my ex was living high off the hog? Thoughts of everything that was right with Cooper's life and wrong with mine played over in my mind like the real-life nightmare that it was. And suddenly, it didn't matter anymore, none of it.

"To hell with it." I tossed another pill into my mouth and washed it down with the final glass of wine. If they found me unconscious, and had to pump my stomach, any woman whose heart had been broken would understand.

The bottle was nearly empty when I reached for it again. I couldn't focus on that; I needed to find my sanctuary. I brought the bottle to my lips and tilted my head back. Once I drained it, I released a deep breath and hoped for the best.

How to get more Vicodin was my only concern. I needed more pills because I had the feeling there'd be more days like the one I'd just experienced. And there was no way I'd be able to handle it all alone.

Minutes later, in the distance, I heard my cell phone ring. It couldn't have been anyone but Yesterday who only wanted to bitch at me for not answering her call earlier.

Why didn't she understand that I didn't want to talk about Cooper's fabulous new life? My life was a shit show compared to his.

The feeling moved slowly, but I felt it coming. Without any warning, the smile made its way to my face, and I couldn't stop it if I tried. This was the feeling I needed. It was warm, but at the same time, gave me a chill that seemed to rush through my veins. The wave of euphoria slowly rained down on me and felt like sheer bliss that began at the top of my head and flowed along the length of my entire body.

Then, without warning, my legs felt like overcooked noodles that threatened to give out on me. I wobbled slightly. I didn't mind; nothing bothered me. The pain was gone, and I was happy.

These days, happiness was something I could only find after my special cocktail. Vicodin and wine had been my only true friends during my hard times.

When I laughed, I pulled a hand up to my chin to wipe the trail of drool that slid down my chin. This time, when I fell back onto the sofa, everything was just fine. I had finally found the happiness I needed, and it felt really good.

The sensation that washed over me felt divine. I felt great, and the more my special cocktail took over, the better I felt—finally.

Boom.

Boom.

It wasn't until I heard my name that I realized someone was at the door. When my good feeling took over, nothing else mattered.

My body wanted to get up and rush to the door, but I couldn't muster up the strength.

Maybe if I closed my eyes, they'd go away. Who was tryna mess up my high and why?

My eyelids felt heavy, and my heart felt light. But still, I found pleasure in everything, the way I breathed, with my chest slowly rising and falling, the way my skin tingled like I was covered with a blanket made of little bolts of electricity. My cocktail was doing its job.

The knock at the door sounded more like the battering ram after a while. They were determined to get in, even if it meant breaking down the front door.

"Could you fucking not!" I yelled at the door.

Warm drool slid down the side of my mouth again, but I didn't care. I felt good. There was no pain, and no worries in my life, except at my front door.

"Open the damn door!" Yesterday yelled.

Experience had taught me she would never go away. I had to choose between my blissful high and the misery I was certain she had on the other side of the door.

Slowly, I dragged myself in its direction and took baby steps hoping she'd get tired and leave. I knew that was highly unlikely.

"I'm not leaving until you open the damn door!" she yelled.

I knew she meant every single word, so I made it to the door, took a deep breath, and pulled it open.

"Shit, Felicia, are you high again?" she asked.

Chapter Five

When Yesterday walked in, the look on her face said she was either surprised by the sight of me, my place or maybe both. I could imagine that after salivating over Coop's crib on TV, mine had to be a huge letdown. She glanced around—and that didn't take long because my place was smaller than a matchbox—then she focused on me.

"What the hell is wrong with you?"

I wasn't sure if she really expected an answer.

"Shhhiiiit, nothing now."

Even the sound of my voice was like bliss. It felt like it came out in a whimsical singsongy tone that anyone could appreciate.

"I can't believe you. Why you got yourself all locked up in this place, high as the moon and all alone?"

I wanted to tell her that should have been the best high ever, and she was messing it up. When I moved, I stumbled a little but caught my balance.

"See, this a damn shame. So, what set you off this time?"

She didn't need to be looking after me; it would've been so much better if she left. Especially the way she was talking to me, I didn't give a damn what she thought, didn't care what Cooper thought. I just wanted to ride my wave in peace and enjoy the blissful feeling. I knew from experience that it wouldn't last forever.

"I told you I wasn't in the mood."

That didn't sound as good as the first words, but she needed to be warned.

"Girl, you don't feel that?"

Yesterday's face twisted as she looked at mine. I wanted to tell her what I did feel, felt good, and it would be much better if she left so I could really enjoy it. Instead, I shook my head. Or at least I thought I did.

Seconds later, her long nails were snapping in front of my eyes.

"You are really messed up right now."

That's what she thought, but I couldn't think of a time when I had felt better. I wasn't addicted to Vicodin and wine, but when I had a hard time, my special cocktail helped soften it, even if a little. Suddenly, her hands were on my arms, and she gently guided me to a seat.

My head began to feel heavy, and I wanted to relax. I didn't need to be examined, didn't need to be scolded, and I didn't even want to talk.

"We need to get you some help. You can't keep doing this to yourself."

The sour expression on my face had more to do with Yesterday's hypocrisy, than the chemical imbalance I had been enjoying. Now she was worried about me and wanted to get me some help?

"Whhhaaat? Talk to me; what's going on?"

"What's going on is you up in here acting all concerned and worried, but yet every chance you get, you rubbing Coop's success in my face. If you not jamming to his damn music, you wanna be talking about his new place with me, like none of that pisses me off."

Yesterday's eyes grew wide. She actually looked surprised.

"What makes you think I need to be discussing a tour of his mansion with you? Why I need to be on the phone while you swooning and creaming over all his nice things? The very damn things that he should've been sharing with me."

By the time I was finished, Yesterday's mouth literally hung wide.

"Girl, what's really wrong with you?"

For a second, I thought I might have been getting through to her. Her expression changed from wonderment and softened, or so I thought.

But suddenly, her neck began to twist.

"So now that you high on pills and liquor, you mistaking that for courage and think you can talk to me all out the side of your mouth?"

Yesterday really was messing up my high, and I needed her to know that. It wasn't about the way I talked to her; it was the way her antics made me feel. But it was clear she wasn't ready to receive what I was saying.

"So just because Coop a star now, you gon' act like you got one foot in the grave? What happened to the Felicia who made all of that possible for him? I don' already told your ass what I thought you should do. You let that man take everything from you. He took your money, your blood, and everything else... what's next? You gonna let him have your life too?"

My eyebrow inched upward at her questions.

"Felicia, ever since you got put out, you been doing just enough to get by. I'm not even gonna say enough to survive, because I ain't seen you do nothing for yourself since he left. But yet, you mad at him and Evelyn. Why you mad? They only did to you what you allowed them to do."

She moved away.

The second I thought she'd finally decided to leave, we both turned toward the knock at the door.

"Damn," Yesterday hissed. She rushed to the door before I could say anything. "I totally forgot," she muttered as she walked over and pulled the door open.

My mother, Tabitha, was always heard before she was seen. If I didn't want to wring Yesterday's neck before, I definitely wanted to now. She had gone and called my messy, phony mama?

"Well, so, is the chile alive or what?" my mother said more than asked as she pranced into my small space. "Fix it, Jesus! Fix it!" she hollered, as she looked around the apartment.

"Hey, Tabitha," Yesterday muttered. "How are you?"

"Hey, chile. I am saved, sanctified, and filled with the Holy Ghost," my mother said.

My eye-roll was so dramatic, I was stunned the balls didn't pop from their sockets. I still couldn't fathom that Yesterday had gone and called my meddling, fake, sanctified momma.

When Cooper became a star, her life had also changed. I had more gray in my hair than you'd ever find in hers. She was once a size 28, but by the time she had her gastric sleeve, tummy-tuck, and complete body lift, she was a curvy size 12. Today, she strutted into my place wearing an expensive-looking brown St. John pants suit, like it was made specifically for her body. The leather of her camel-colored designer handbag looked delicately soft. He had bought my mama, and she showed no shame in accepting everything he tossed her way.

Tabitha clutched her purse closer to her body as she scanned the room. I was certain she had spotted everything that was wrong, within seconds. I watched in horror as she flung her head back and began her rant.

"Every single day, I fall to my knees and beg the good Lord to do something to help this child of mine." Her face couldn't even hide the disdain. She turned to me and said, "So what! You lost your man. You ain't the first, and sure ain't gonna be the last woman to experience that, Lord knows. I ain't been saved all my life. I've been there before."

Confirmation that my high was gone came the second my

mother pivoted in her red-bottoms and moved toward the window. She glanced out, frowned, and turned back to us.

"I don't see how you continue to carry on like this," she said. "Umph, umph, umph, we're living in our last days for sure!"

Yesterday's eyes quickly shifted to the floor. She didn't dare look at me; she knew I was beyond pissed. My relationship with my mother had taken a turn when things had started to fall apart with Coop and me, but when she had taken his and Evelyn's side, that pretty much did us in. The money and gifts were enticing, but she'd sold me out, and we all knew it.

"I keep telling you," my mother began.

"I know, let go and let God," I repeated nearly in unison with her, but with far less enthusiasm.

She looked at me, her brows knitted in confusion.

"Blasphemy! Blasphemy!" she hollered.

There was nothing my mother could say or do for me, and she knew it. Everyone else might have bought her phony persona with all of the religious sayings and biblical references, but I knew better.

"I'ma keep praying for you, chile. I'ma keep praying because the devil is a lie if he thinks I'm giving up my child without a fight."

Chapter Six

"Wheeew!" My mother struggled to take off her designer shoes. "These suckers may be expensive, but they are nothing nice on my feet."

Yesterday and I watched as she took a pair of ballerina flats from her bag and eased the red-bottom pumps to the side. I struggled to contain the eye-roll that was itching to escape.

My mother straightened herself, then looked away from me.

"Yesterday, I need a word with you in the hall," she said. Relief returned to my senses, and I got hopeful. Could they finally be leaving?

Yesterday looked at me with sorrowful eyes, but she and my mother turned away.

My high felt like it was about to come back when they stepped outside. I quickly locked the door behind them. Once alone, my thoughts instantly traveled back to the beginning, when the future looked so bright for Cooper and me.

"Baby, you have such a beautiful voice, I just know you can make it."

"Licia, you've been saying that longer than we've been married now. You know I like singing for you, the fam, and friends, but to say I can make a living doing it?" He shrugged.

Cooper knew his talent was real and enough of us told him continuously. At times, it was like he wanted to hear it over and over again. Because I suspected as much, I stroked his ego more than I did most things.

I was pregnant with our son, and moving around had become

real uncomfortable. Cooper was more attentive than ever, and it made me want to do whatever might keep him happy. Even if that meant constantly reinforcing what he already knew. Cooper was very talented.

"Coop, do you hear yourself? If you're good enough to sing at all those doggone family functions, including funerals, why wouldn't you be able to make a living doing it?"

He didn't answer. He shrugged slightly, but I could tell he was giving serious thought to what I said. Many professionals were not as good as him.

Cooper got up and walked over to the mirror that hung near the door. He stared at his reflection. He did that a lot. Sometimes I felt like he thought he had settled in life. Cooper was a very good-looking man with a voice that was angelic. We had met in high school during a talent show and had been inseparable ever since.

After a four-year stint in the Army, he came back to Houston and got a job driving Metro buses. It wasn't the best job for a man who had dreams of stardom, but it was good enough.

"Oh." I adjusted myself on the sofa.

Cooper turned away from his reflection, and looked at me. "My boy acting up again, huh?" He moved closer.

Once I placed my hand on my belly, the baby seemed to settle. "You doing good, baby, you doing good. We only got a few more weeks to go, and it'll be over."

I closed my eyes and prayed the baby would come on time. I was tired of being pregnant. I wanted my old body back. I needed to feel like myself again.

Within seconds, Cooper kneeled down next to me.

"I sing because I'm happy...

I sing because I'm free...

For his eye is on the sparrow…"

His voice seemed to calm the baby even more. I closed my eyes and allowed the sound of his voice to carry me away. I loved when Cooper sang. Usually, he'd sing some Luther or Barry White, but when he sang to my stomach and our son, he always sang an old gospel song.

Within seconds, I felt myself relax, and that's when the idea came to me. I knew Cooper would make it as a professional singer. He had the voice, the look, and the determination.

My eyes snapped open.

"Let's do it, baby."

Cooper stopped singing and turned to face me.

"Woman, what you talking about? We can't do nothing until you drop this load."

He gently rubbed my stomach, and we watched as a small foot stretched outward.

"This boy is real active," Cooper said. He beamed with pride as we watched the baby move around.

"I know I can't do much now, but the baby is due in a couple of weeks. After that, I think you should let me manage your career."

Cooper's eyebrow went up. It seemed as if the idea were somewhat enticing.

"What career? I don't need a manager to tell me how to sit behind that wheel every day, baby."

We laughed.

"Yeah, I know that, but if you ever hope to live your true dream of hitting it big as a singer and entertainer, you need to let me manage your career."

His eyes locked with mine, and I saw the true depth of his curiosity. He was still battling self-doubt, but he was warming up to the idea, and he was truly curious about what might be possible.

"What you know about managing careers?"

"I'll admit, I don't know much, but it's like when I used to manage Eve in those gawd-awful pageants she loved so much. Baby, I could do the same for you. I'll use the time to do some research, figure out whether we should go into the studio ourselves, drop some of your work on social media, let it go viral; then things could really take off."

Cooper fell back onto his butt. He leaned back on extended arms, then gazed up at the ceiling for a long time.

"How would that work?"

"Honey, couples do it all the time. Who better to manage you than the one person who loves and believes in you? You know for sure that I'll do anything to help you make it, and I'll do everything to make sure you get out there and get the recognition you deserve."

Cooper sighed. He shook his head slightly.

"But what do you know about managing anything?"

The first time he'd asked, it didn't bother me as much. It sounded like a common-sense question, but now that it was a serious conversation, and he still felt like that, made me wonder about whether he believed I could do it.

"Baby, you and the entire entertainment industry probably can't compare to a bunch of backstabbing, catty, beauty-queen wannabes. Trust when I tell you, they can get downright vicious, and if I survived them, I can handle a bunch of music executives." Cooper stared at me for a long while.

"I dunno, Licia."

He may have been unsure, but his demeanor made me feel like the possibility might have excited him a little.

"Think about it. Just hear me out. If I can't get you a few gigs, and we're not making any progress after about six months, we can find someone else."

He didn't look completely convinced.

"I can get you some local gigs to start with. Then, once we make you a star here at home, in your own backyard, we can take it on the road."

"So you'd be able to get me gigs?"

I could tell by his tone that the idea was one he wanted to explore.

"Baby, I'll get you gigs, we'll cut a demo, and we will make this happen. But first," my headed tilted ever so slightly in his direction, "you've gotta get on board."

"Can I think about it?"

My heart sank a little at that response, but I wasn't about to give up. "What's there to think about? You say you want to be a star, and I'm saying let's do it, but now you seem to be backtracking. So, what is it; do you or don't you wanna be a star, baby?"

Cooper stared at me for a moment, and silence hung between us.

"You real serious about this, huh?" Cooper still looked at me like he was struggling to believe.

"I don't see why you're not."

He stared harder at me.

But after a while, a sudden and deliberate grin slowly spread across his face. His dimples deepened and he nodded.

"What the hell; let's do this!"

"So, we're doing this? Oh, shit!"

Fear settled into his features.

"What?"

I looked down, tried to steady my breathing, and said, "I think it's time; my water just broke!"

Chapter Seven

Three years after I'd agreed to manage Coop's singing career, we were deep in the struggle, and the true battle was mine alone.

Cooper had become such a diva, I had to remind myself to keep my eyes on the bigger picture. A lot of the work involved the type of things I wasn't good at doing: begging someone to give him a shot, or begging for the honorarium or check we were promised after he had already preformed. It was infuriating.

The biggest challenge was chasing down our money if we didn't get it the night of the performance. I thought about this as a voice rang through the cell phone. It was my third time calling, and I was frustrated.

"I need to talk to the person who pays the bills, that's who I need to talk to," I screamed into the phone. My patience was ultra-thin.

Cooper had done a gig out at Sam Houston Race Park and we hadn't gotten paid. I usually required payment the night of, and in cash, but I also didn't like to turn down opportunities when people couldn't or wouldn't agree to those terms. We had done work out at the park before, but this time, getting paid was nearly impossible. And we needed every dime of our money.

"Hold on; let me get my manager," the woman said.

As I waited, my mind raced with the list of other things that needed my attention.

"Felicia, this is Andrew. Listen, I'm sorry about all of this, but you really need to talk with the vendor we used. That was a third-party event. Our facility was rented for it. So, what you're gonna have to do is track down the vendor and call them up. We've paid all of our bills. The rest, including Coop's, has nothing to do with us."

Andrew Kiner was a slick businessman who did several events around the city. He looked like an old school gangster, but he was a man of his word. I knew that for sure; we had done business with him for nearly a year. And he always looked out for us; he was fair.

"Listen, I know this won't help, but we don't plan to use that vendor anymore. You're the fourth person having problems getting paid."

"Damn, Andrew, why would y'all use somebody like that in the first place?"

"Aey, over here, the boss is only interested in business. Who am I to say no? You know how it can be sometimes."

I understood his position, but I hated to have to beg for money we had already earned, needed and should have had.

"So what do you think I should do? We need that money." I was pissed to learn that once again, I'd have to chase down some money that we'd worked to earn. The craziest part was, I couldn't let Cooper know what was going on because he'd trip out on me. He'd blame me for not predicting that someone wouldn't pay; then he'd threaten to have me replaced, yet again.

"A few people have gone down to their office. They're over on the Southwest side. I can find the address, if you've got a minute."

"I've looked them up and thought they were on the Northside, near you guys." I was confused. I didn't want to admit to Andrew that I had already been by their offices, without any luck, so I waited for him to find the correct address.

"Nah, don't waste your time going out there. That's another

office; let me grab the one you need. Oh, before I forget, I wanted to tell you about something. My wife's kinfolk got this club, and they try to bring in live music every Friday. I think Coop would be a good fit."

My heart started to race.

"It's a club?" I tried not to sound as desperate as I really was. I'd been working for a while to try and land a regular gig for Cooper. A weekly gig would be perfect; he'd get the regular practice and incredible exposure.

"Yeah, nothing too fancy, but he gets lots of traffic through there, and you never know whom you could meet."

When he said those words, it confirmed that we clearly thought alike, and that was a good thing.

"Oh for sure, for sure. Who do I need to talk to?"

"Okay, slow down a bit. Let me give you the bad news. This dude ain't like me or the people you work with out here. He's not the type you want to meet in a dark alley."

Andrew's message was clear enough, but my need for a regular gig outweighed the warning and even any potential danger. Besides, I knew how to avoid dark alleys.

"You know I can hold my own," I joked.

"Yeah, since I've watched you work over the last year, I felt like you could handle Big Al. He's something else. And whatever you do, negotiate with him."

Before I got off the phone, I had the information I needed for Andrew's brother-in-law and the address I needed to go get our money.

Four days later, I dropped Cooper off at work before daybreak; then I drove to the address Andrew had given me. It was still dark outside, and that's just the way I wanted it. I had tried everything. I had called, stopped by in the morning, during lunch, and near the end of the business day. Each time I came to the office, it looked boarded up, like no one had been there. But I knew better.

One day, I even called Andrew back to double-check the address. Once he confirmed it was correct, I decided I needed a different approach, and I knew what had to be done.

The nondescript office was located in a strip mall off Westheimer and the Beltway. There was no sign on the door. Next to the small office was a cell phone repair store; next to that, a Chinese fast-food restaurant and a couple of empty spaces with "For Lease" signs taped on doors.

Several people, mostly women, rushed from their cars and into the various businesses as the sun made an appearance. I was getting antsy as I waited. Traffic between workers and customers grew and slowed, but no one showed up at the address I'd been watching.

When my cell phone rang, I was irritated that the stakeout was taking longer than I wanted. It was my mother, so I needed to answer.

"Hey," I greeted.

"Where you at?"

"I'm handling some business; is everything okay?"

My mother watched Trey for us during the day. She worked a part-time job in the evening, so between my schedule and Cooper's, we were good. But there were times when my mother felt like I should take the baby, if I wasn't at my job.

"Umph, what kind of business you handling this time of morning?"

If she could have seen my face, she would've been able to detect the irritation her question had caused.

"Ma, I'm really busy right now; is everything okay with Trey?"

"Yeah, he's fine. I'm just wondering where you are and what you're doing. You left the house so early, I was just checking on you."

"I told you, I'm handling some business. Look, I need to run. I'll be back in a few hours."

"You never said where you are," she said. I ignored her question again.

"Okay, I'll call you when I'm on my way back."

Before I ended the call, I heard her suck her teeth. But I couldn't focus on that. I finally saw someone walk up to the office door and unlock it.

The man looked like he had seen a few unexpected visitors before. As he put the key into the lock, he looked around almost nervously.

My mind raced with thoughts of how I'd handle this situation. I didn't want any crap, but I needed our money.

Early January in Houston could be anything from near summerlike temperatures to full-blown winter days. On this day, it felt more like spring, so the trench coat I wore over my jeans, boots, and T-shirt was the perfect cover I needed, and could have been appropriate in case a sudden thunderstorm struck. Before I approached the building, I went to the trunk and grabbed the tire iron.

By the time I reached the door, I barged in like someone owed me money, and I was there to collect by any means necessary. His mistake of not locking the door would be his downfall.

The petite man who whipped around at the sound of the door opening looked like I had caught him off guard. And that was exactly the way I wanted it. I swung the tire iron across the desk and watched his eyes grow as items flew across the room and crashed to the floor.

"My next swing will be straight at your motherfucking head!"

Horror was all over his face.

He flinched.

"Lady, I'm calling the police!"

"You're gonna need more than just the police, so I suggest you beg for an ambulance, too, while you're on the phone."

His eyes danced around me, and I didn't know if he were looking for a weapon or what he was thinking.

I took the tire iron and swung it at the desk. The wood crushed on contact.

"While you're on the phone with the cops, tell them how I've been calling, leaving notes and literally chasing down your thieving behind for weeks."

I lifted the tire iron again, and slowly his hands went up in surrender. "Okay, okay, let's talk about this. How much?"

"Five hundred and I need cash!"

"Crazy woman!" he muttered. But he dug into his back pocket and pulled out a large billfold.

With shaky hands, he opened it and pulled out a thick wad of cash. He counted out the bills and then looked up at me when he ran out at $487.

"This is all I got right now," he said.

I snatched the stack of bills from the desk, and then examined it with one hand. "Consider us even. Use the rest to pay for the damages."

He started going off in a language I didn't understand, but he stayed away from me. I glanced around, pivoted, pulled the tire iron close, and strolled out of the small office, cash in hand.

Chapter Eight

"Hi, Big Al, this is Felicia Malone calling again. I'd like to come by and talk to you about my client. Please give me a call when you get this message."

The message I'd left for Big Al was vague enough for him to wonder whether we'd done business before and maybe get him to call back. That was my hope because I didn't have another plan.

By the time I made it to the bank later that afternoon, I was disgusted. Cooper didn't know what I'd had to do to get the money, but he knew how to spend it.

We needed all kinds of things, but he was quick to put his needs before the family's. Something had told me to check our balance before I deposited the money, and I was glad I had.

I snatched the phone and dialed Cooper's cell phone. I knew he wouldn't answer because drivers had to keep their cell phones stashed away while they were on their routes. He usually got a break around two, and he'd get my message then.

"What the hell did you buy this time? We are overdrawn by three-hundred damn dollars! Cooper, I told you, check before you spend! We've got several charges on here because of over-draft fees! Damn!"

My eyes focused on the cash I held in my hands. There was no way I wanted to turn all of that cash over to the bank after all I'd gone through to get it.

I walked away from the bank feeling defeated. It seemed the harder I worked, the less progress we made. Cooper's spending was reckless, and there was little I could do to control it. He spent more money than he brought in, and he did it regularly.

My mother allowed us to stay in her garage apartment as long as we paid for the utilities and a small amount for rent. She called it a garage apartment, but it was not detached from the house, so it felt more like a spare bedroom.

She could get a whole lot more if she sealed off the connecting door and rented at market, but she was trying to help us out.

Cooper's check covered the rent and most bills, but his vice of tailored clothes, fine shoes, and other accessories was what had killed us.

"Licia, I gotta look the part. I can't buy suits off the rack at Macy's; my shit's got to say I'm a star!"

Instead of focusing on how pissed I was at Cooper, I went to the grocery store and bought some food. The last thing I wanted was for my mother to bitch and complain about us not pulling our weight.

By the time I'd finished with the errands, I had $50 left. I put $30 of that into my mother's gas tank and drove her car back to the house. I knew she'd be waiting with lots of questions. I'd deal with Cooper and his spending later.

My mother was in the kitchen hovering over a pot, and my son was planted in front of the TV.

"Hey, where you been all morning?" she asked.

"I had to pay some bills and run to the store. I noticed we were running low on a few things."

The slight eye-twitch would have been easy to miss, but I caught it. My mother liked having Trey around most times, but I knew there were other times when she probably wished we had our own place. She walked over and peered into one of the bags I had placed on the counter.

"Oh, you didn't have to do that. I know things are tight for you guys right now. Bless your heart; you bought me some pecan ice cream?"

"Yeah, I heard you fussing at Trey about it the other day," I said.

"I wouldn't say I was fussing; you know how that boy is. I tried to give him a taste; next thing you know, he don' ate the whole doggone pint!"

We chuckled about my son. But the truth was, between Trey and Cooper, we always ran out of milk, juice, bread, and any kind of snack that came into the house.

"What are you fixing? It smells good."

"My famous chili."

My mother looked out of the kitchen window. "I know it's winter, despite what the sunshine says, so I thought a good pot of chili would be perfect."

"Ma, can you watch Trey Friday night? I'm working on a gig for Coop, and we need to go check out the club."

"Chile, no problem; you know I'm pulling for y'all, so anything I can do to help."

I had no doubt that she meant what she said, but I also knew it had to be hard to have us up under her for as long as we had been staying there.

My mother told me she wanted to take a nap before she had to leave for her shift, so that meant I needed to handle my son. I figured I'd catch up on some paperwork, and try to follow up with several leads that could turn into gigs for Cooper.

After she scooped some of the ice cream into a bowl, my mother took a few catalogs from the kitchen counter and went to her room.

Trey was fully mesmerized by the cartoons on TV. I was about to go and get him when my phone rang. As Coop's manager, I couldn't afford to miss a call. We never knew when the game-changing call would come through, and I needed to answer.

"This is Felicia Malone," I answered.

"Big Al here," his deep voice said.

"Oh, yes, Big Al, thanks for calling me back. Like I said on my message, I'm trying to see if we can get an audition. One of my clients would be a perfect fit for your club."

Since it was so quiet on the other end, I wasn't sure if Al had hung up.

"Al, you still there?" I asked.

"Yeah. I'm good. But peep this. C'mon by the club tomorrow at three."

"Uh, tomorrow?"

My mind quickly ran over whether I had anything to do the next day. I couldn't think fast enough, and nothing important came to mind.

"I'm not sure Coop can take off on such short notice; he drives for Metro and—"

"I said *you* come by the club. After I talk with you, I'll let you know if I wanna see your client."

Big Al cut me off. His voice was deep and powerful. He didn't say much, and what little he said was pretty straightforward.

"Tomorrow at three," he repeated.

Something didn't feel right. Of course I was going to go, but I needed him to hear Cooper sing. There was no point in me going alone when I was trying to push Coop.

Releasing a deep breath, I decided I'd keep an open mind and wait to see what happened when I met with Big Al.

Chapter Nine

The actress who cracked up with wild laughter on TV brought me back to the nightmare I was still experiencing. When I used to watch the tabloid TV shows, they left me feeling like a failure. Back in the day, I used to think if only I could book Coop on one of those, then the world would see what I knew.

He had a great voice, and he looked good; that would get us by because his attitude was shit. But my hope was, people would fall in love with the voice and the lyrics before they ever got to know the real asshole he was. That was my strategy.

I swung my feet to the floor. The last thing I needed to do was spend my day on memory lane. While Coop was living the good life, I was still picking up the pieces.

When the loud knock sounded at the door, I ignored it. I wanted Yesterday and my mother to leave. I was done with the conversation and didn't want them looking at me with pitiful eyes.

"Felicia! Open the doggone door!" Yesterday screamed from the other side.

The noise they were kicking up was loud, but it meant nothing to me. If I ignored them long enough, I hoped they'd leave.

I glanced over at the red-bottoms that seemed to taunt me from their spot on floor. My mother and I didn't wear the same size shoes, and I couldn't think of a time when I'd be able to spend more than $1,000 on a single pair of shoes.

"Felicia! Open up!" Yesterday said sternly.

Why did she still think she could bully me with a locked door between us? The moment she called my mother over, she should have known all negotiations were over. My mother was just another reminder of all I had lost when Cooper had left.

"I'm about to take a nap. I'll talk with you later," I said.

There was more knocking. Then, for a few seconds, it stopped.

"Oooh wee!" I heard my mother say. "She'd better be glad I'm saved! Oooh wee; oooh weee!"

If only she knew I didn't give a hot damn about her being saved. For that comment, she wasn't getting her damn shoes back. I plucked them from the floor and placed them into my closet. My mother had shown me what really mattered when she'd chosen Evelyn and Cooper's side.

For all I cared, she and Yesterday could fall off somewhere, and I wouldn't be the least bit pressed. Funny how now, all of a sudden, they were so concerned about my well-being.

People loved to linger and gawk at wreckage after an accident. It was almost like my pathetic life somehow made them feel more secure in their own. Well, enough with the rubbernecking; it was time to move on!

"Felicia, I know you're mad, but we care about you. We want you to get better. And that's the only reason I called Miss Tabitha. She's still your mother, and I wish you would let us back in, so we can talk to you about what's going on here."

The only thing that would make me better was another cocktail. But I was out of wine and intentionally didn't remember where any more Vicodin pills were stashed.

The knocks started up again. I wanted them to stop and go away.

Neither of them could say anything I wanted to hear. They had blown my high, and traces of my cocktail were nowhere to be found in my system. I was completely sober and knew for sure there was nothing I could do to get that blissful feeling back.

Yesterday was crazy if she thought I was about to unlock the door and let them back in. I couldn't stand them while I was under the influence. Now that I was sober, my patience was even thinner.

"Felicia, just let us talk for a few more minutes," she pleaded.

My eyes had rolled so much, they were tired. There was nothing they could say to make me want to open the door. I needed them to get the hint and leave. I thought my mother would ask for her expensive shoes, but she didn't.

"Ooh wee, the devil is busy!" said my mother. "That ol' devil sho'nuff is on his J-O-B today!"

She sounded like she would break out in full-blown, Holy-Ghost-induced, shouting church-woman testimony any second.

As the two of them banged on my door and pleaded with me to let them back in, all I could think about was how Yesterday continued to betray the trust that was supposed to exist between best friends.

Not only did she continuously talk about Coop and his new successful career, but for her to reach out to my mother, knowing the state of *our* relationship, it made me wonder about her true loyalty to our friendship. It wasn't the drugs talking because this thought was nothing new for me.

"Felicia, c'mon, open the door!"

The pleas were followed by knocks, and they were working my nerves. It seemed like they got louder.

Suddenly, another voice joined the chorus.

"Aey, aey, what's going on here?"

That was my landlord, Mr. Belton. He reminded me of a person who might have been in the witness protection program. He rarely left the building, hardly ever had company, and only spoke when it was necessary. The lines on his face gave him a permanent sagging expression. He kept a short, unlit, but burnt cigar in the corner of his mouth, and he moved at his own pace, regardless of the urgency. I wondered why it had taken him so long to question them about the noise, because he seldom tolerated any type of disturbance in our small building. He once had said, "If it's quiet, there's no need to call the law."

"My daughter is in there, and I think she's in danger," I heard my mother say.

Oh the theatrics! I frowned. But I knew Mr. Belton well enough to know she'd have to come harder and better than that.

"What kind of danger?" Mr. Belton asked. I imagined he was very unimpressed with my mother's plea.

"We think she may be suicidal," my mother lied.

That's when I rushed close to the door and leaned against it to get a better listen. It was funny how she could just put her religion on the shelf when it suited her. She had just told a bold-faced lie, and she knew it. Yesterday knew it too, but she didn't say anything.

"I'm far from suicidal. I just want to be left the hell alone. I don't want to be bothered," I yelled.

At first, there was complete silence. I wasn't sure what was going on out there. But it didn't take long for the rumbling to start.

"Ah, okay, that's it; you ladies need to leave," Mr. Belton said.

"Wait, just give us a few more minutes," Yesterday pleaded.

"Nah; y'all need to go! People starting to complain. She said she don't want to be bothered, so I need y'all to go."

"Felicia, you gonna let your mama get tossed out on the streets like this?" I heard my mother ask.

"Ain't nobody tossing nobody out. I'm saying y'all need to leave," my landlord repeated. This time his voice was firmer, and it sounded like he was about to go off.

"In the name of Jesus, I need you to unlock this door, so we can look in on my child before you force us out," she finally demanded.

It was obvious Mr. Belton was not swayed.

"Ma'am, you can call on God himself, but I'm here to tell you, that ain't gonna happen. I need the two of you to leave," he insisted.

"This here is a welfare check. I'm telling you there's something wrong with my child!" my mother continued.

"Felicia, you're just gonna let it go down like this?" Yesterday asked.

"You can call the police and they'll help you conduct a real welfare check, but for now, I've heard from the tenant. She says she's fine and wants to be left alone. C'mon, let's get to moving!" Mr. Belton said.

Upon hearing my landlord tell them to get the police, I walked away from the door. The truth was, I didn't give a damn what happened. They had ruined my high and left me in a real funky mood. I hoped the landlord tossed them both out, and if it took him too long, I might call the cops and complain myself.

I grabbed a bottle of water, went back to the couch, and flopped down. After a few minutes, I eased back and thought about all I had done for Cooper.

The thoughts came so quickly, it was like they'd never left my mind.

Although I had waited with great anticipation for Coop to get home to talk about my upcoming meeting with Big Al, he wasn't in the mood.

"You don't think we need to discuss it?" I asked as I drove us home.

"Licia, you're the manager; you do what you have to and I don't need to know about every step you take. Just make it happen."

For the rest of the drive, I listened to music while Cooper talked on his cell phone. My mind was on overdrive with how I would convince Big Al that Cooper needed to be his next new star. I felt like our future depended on me landing that gig for him. Cooper couldn't bother himself with the actual details of business; he only wanted to be in the spotlight.

"Dawg, I woulda told him, I can't put you in no pussy, and I can't keep you out of it."

At the sound of his conversation, I turned and looked at him. Cooper was oblivious to my presence as he talked to his boy on the phone. He couldn't ever pretend to show respect.

"Sounds to me like she just trying to get her body count up. I mean, if he love her, I wouldn't say nothing, but between me and you, that shit ain't cool." He chuckled. "Shiiid, she couldn't be mine. Not like that. Baby, if you out there giving it up, you need to drop my last name is how I look at it."

To me, this was a good time for us to strategize about our plan for his career. But instead, Cooper caught up on the phone calls he couldn't make during the day. Most of the calls were to his loser friends who couldn't do anything to help advance his career. But what could I say? When it came to his career, Cooper felt like it was all on me, and a part of me agreed. As his manager, it was my job to set him up nicely. But it would've been nice to have his help and some of his support. His words stayed with me long after they were spoken.

"If I go around begging to play a venue or negotiating for a gig that diminishes my status. It's almost like people can't see me as the star I am because they'll remember I had to beg to get the gig in the first place." He shook his head. "Licia, that's not a good look."

The more I thought about what he said, the more I agreed. I didn't mind doing the begging and groveling. In the end, any win on my part was a win for our family. But Cooper could do something to help. As it stood, he simply sat back and waited to see what if anything I could produce.

As I had listened to Cooper's phone call about his boy's woman who had been caught cheating, there was no way I could have begun to imagine all I'd have to do to help jumpstart my husband's career.

Chapter Ten

Hours after we were home and settled, my cell phone rang. I didn't even want to look and see who was calling. So many of the calls were about things or services I could buy. I needed some paying gigs. We didn't have money to spend unless that money was going to morph and double or triple overnight, and none of those calls could produce those type of results.

The next day, after I'd dropped Cooper at work, I decided to kill a little time before my meeting with Big Al. There was lots to do in Houston, but the problem was, almost everything required spending money. I needed ways to generate income, not spend money we really couldn't spare.

After lots of consideration, I decided to go to the library. There, I could get a list of the live music venues around the city and try to find a residency for Cooper. I didn't want any of the 'hood places because that would lead to problems. Cooper needed to mingle in the upscale places where someone influential might stumble in and witness his talent. That was what we needed to get things really popping for his career.

The central library downtown was closer since I had just dropped Cooper off. The first obstacle I faced was parking. It made no sense to me that there was no free, easy parking to access the city's main library.

Driving in downtown Houston was nowhere on my list of favorite things to do. I took Walker Street and made a left onto Bagby Street, and horns started blaring. The sudden noise threatened to send my nervous system into shock.

"Oh shit, this is a one-way!" I muttered as I realized my error. Driving downtown always confused me. It was hard to navigate the one-ways and all the other confusing stuff going on. After a quick adjustment, I rode Walker another block up, made the left, then turned onto Bagby.

By the time I saw the library, my nerves were so frazzled, I didn't even want to look for free parking on the street. I pulled into the underground garage and tried to catch my breath. Since two dollars was all I could spare, I quickly left the car. I had an hour before the price of parking would go up.

As I walked into the massive building, the crisp air conditioning cooled me instantly, and I finally felt some relief.

"Good morning, how can I help you today?" an older woman with silver hair greeted me from behind the information desk.

After I told her what I wanted, she told me the sections I needed and gave me a slip of paper with information she had written down to help me.

"Thank you."

As I turned to leave, she called after me. "Ma'am," she said. "Actually, might I suggest another idea?"

I returned to the information desk to hear her out. "The library is fine, but I think the tourist and visitor center across the street at city hall would probably serve you better."

She ended her suggestion with a half shrug. Those were the type of things that made me want to kick myself. She was so correct. While I could look places up at the library, it would probably be easier and more efficient to go to the visitor center, because that's where I'd find the most current information about events happening around the city. That was the way I needed my brain to work without having to be told. It was going to take critical, clever thinking to make progress with Cooper's career.

"Oooh, but I parked over here. Should I move my car?"

"No, this parking lot serves both buildings."

Instead of going to the reference areas she'd jotted down on the piece of paper, I left the library and bolted across the street to city hall. Excitement flooded my system as I thought about all the possibilities that I might find there.

I pulled the large glass doors open and walked into the rotunda. Two ladies wearing badges stood right outside the center's door as I approached.

I eased up and introduced myself. "Hi, I'm Felicia Malone, a local promoter, and I'm trying to find live music venues to book my clients in."

The women smiled, shook my hand, and greeted me with excitement. One woman's eyes literally lit up.

"Oh, my goodness! We were just talking about some of the city's upcoming events. Do you have a card?"

Thank God I did. I dug into my purse and pulled two cards from the shiny little card holder. The women talked to me about a few upcoming events and how I could submit my artists for consideration as opening acts. They also directed me to brochures that listed lounges, restaurants, and bars that hosted live music either weekly or monthly.

They were friendly and offered up lots of useful information.

By the time I arrived back at the underground garage, my parking bill had more than tripled, but I felt like it was worth it. I had lot of information about various downtown and surrounding area venues. Behind the wheel again, I left downtown and headed south. I took the exit off 288 South, and made my way to Dixie Street. My stomach let out a mean growl and for the first time all day, I realized I hadn't eaten a thing. I was on autopilot trying to make something happen for my client.

Low on cash and anxious to land Cooper a gig, I figured I'd use the hunger as fuel to push forward. I knew I was closer than ever.

Silly of me to have thought that arriving at the club to meet Big Al early would be a problem. There was lots of activity surrounding the place as I got out of my car and headed for the door. That gave me hope and made me feel like landing this gig would finally make Cooper hopeful and happy. It would show him that I was fully capable of managing his career and may even inspire him to take a more active role.

As I approached, I watched two men unload a delivery truck. The moment they realized I was there, they stopped and stared until I came closer.

"Hi, I'm here to see Big Al," I greeted. It was awkward the way they stared as I walked.

It took a minute before they spoke, so I wasn't sure whether they had heard me.

"He expecting you?" one man finally asked.

"Yeah, he told me to come by this afternoon."

"Oh, okay; well, he's not here yet."

My heart sank. The expression on my face must've said so, because the guy started patting his pants' pockets and looking around.

"Well, now, hold on a minute, let me call him and find out his ETA. I don't want you getting all upset."

"Oh, no, it's nothing like that. It's just I've had a long day, and this is my last meeting before I'm able to wrap it up." I tried to offer a smile, but I was sure it came across weak and flat. I was hungry and tired. The last thing I wanted to hear was that Al forgot about our meeting after he'd insisted I come by today. I really needed to get this gig for Cooper.

Nearly two hours, and three Cokes later, I sat at the back bar section and still waited. If I had anything else going, I would have left long ago. But this gig would do so much for Cooper and for me. Maybe it would stop him from threatening to replace me.

The ruckus and loud noises going on around me didn't faze me much after hours of waiting. I was frustrated, and I needed Al to come on, so I could grab something to eat.

I looked around the club and had to remind myself that the big picture was what's important.

Milan's color scheme made the place seem busy even when it was nearly empty. There were several sections, but no continuity in the décor, setup, or design. The back bar, where I sat, was done in blue tones with lime-green walls on either side. But then the DJ section had multicolored patterns on the walls, with red cocktail tables and high chairs.

The T-Lounge and the On the Nile sections made me wonder what the place would look like at night. I had been there too long if I'd started questioning the décor and trying to make sense of the place's design. Big Al needed to hurry.

"He must have the live bands over there," I muttered to myself as I looked around. The place was large, but it was old and in need of several upgrades and renovations.

There were zebra-patterned seats, mixed with odd-looking backdrops as walls. Honestly, it looked like someone had found a bunch of mismatched items, thrown them into the large spaces, and called it a club. The venue was far from the upscale surroundings I dreamed of, but still, I waited.

From the moment I'd pulled up outside, I'd convinced myself that none of that would matter if I could get Cooper to perform there as a mainstay. I wouldn't give a damn if the walls had polka-dot and stripes as long as we could call it our musical home.

"You must be Felicia," said a voice so deep, that it gave me the chills. A man's voice did it for me. Some women liked height, some liked weight, and some liked the eyes, but for me, it was all about the voice.

I stumbled as I got up from the high barstool I'd been perched on for nearly three hours and extended a hand. He looked down at me and my hand but couldn't accept it because both of his were full.

He motioned with his head. "C'mon back here to my office."

Al was a big man with a commanding presence. I imagined he shopped at one of those Big and Tall stores. He wore a Kangol Bamboo Ivy cap turned backward, an Oxford shirt with paisley detailing, and a pair of jeans with a starched crease.

It had been a long time since I'd seen a man wear jeans with a crease. Outside of his dated appearance, and even the fact that he literally could change our lives, at that moment, what excited me most was the plastic bag he carried with the other stuff.

The aroma from the chicken woke my senses and made my stomach grumble with pain. Since I hadn't eaten, my stomach was on high alert. I hoped he didn't hear the sound or see the hunger in my eyes for both the food and the gig.

"You want some Frenchy's? I ain't had lunch yet," he said as he sat behind a desk that was larger than his body.

"Oh, my God! I'm so hungry! You sure you wouldn't mind?"

It wasn't professional, but neither were the pictures of half-naked women plastered all over the walls in Big Al's office.

At that point in my reminiscences, I must have drifted off to sleep.

Chapter Eleven

It was close to midnight when my eyes fluttered open. I was instantly frustrated; waking at that time of night, I wouldn't be able to go back to sleep. I had no idea how long Yesterday and my mother had stayed in the hall arguing with my landlord, and I didn't care. They were gone, and that was all that mattered to me.

When I looked at my cell phone and noticed several missed calls, the only one that threatened to send me into full cardiac arrest was the one from my son.

Trey rarely called, and here I had missed him when he finally had. My heart sank at the thought. I put my face into my palms and cried. Cooper didn't even have the decency to make sure our son stayed in touch with me. It was like he'd stripped me of everything that meant anything, and he was okay with it.

In the rare moments when Trey called, he never had much to say to me. I had known how unfair life could be for a very long time, but I never expected things to turn out the way they had after Cooper left. My son was a complete stranger to me, and it hurt that I couldn't do much about it.

It was hard to go from a full house to being alone. Over the last couple of years, I'd struggled with the adjustment, but now that I had to see Cooper's likeness and listen to his voice, it was like reliving the betrayal and breakup all over again.

"What time did he call?" I muttered as I scrolled through my phone's call log. When I realized he had called around 7:30, I hated myself even more. I hadn't heard the phone when it rang.

But the truth was, if I had heard it, I wouldn't have answered. I was trying to ignore calls from Yesterday and my mother, and I never expected to hear from my son.

There was nothing I could do at midnight. I didn't turn on the TV. I lay in the dark and stared at the ceiling. My hope was that I'd fall back to sleep. Instead, my mind was busy with thoughts of the past.

Two weeks after my initial meeting with Big Al, I hadn't heard back from him, and I felt like a complete failure. Cooper and I went there one Friday night, and I hated that I'd even taken him. The frown that invaded his features, when I pulled into the parking lot, never left his face. He found everything wrong with the club and the people there, and what he didn't find, he complained about anyway.

"This place needs to be shut down, completely demolished, then maybe they can reopen, once they've upgraded and rebuilt," he said as he looked around.

I wanted to remind him that no one had asked what he thought. Lately, nothing had been good enough for Cooper. He found fault in everything, and I wondered whether I'd be able to please him.

"You wanted me to perform here?" By now, his face was so squinted up, it was as if his senses were under attack from a foul scent.

I shot him a glance that he ignored as he ranted on. It would've started an argument if I'd pointed out that he wasn't performing anywhere currently, so this would be an actual step up, but I didn't say so.

As he looked around and criticized the setting, the music, and even the wait staff, my eyes and focus were on looking for Big Al. He was nowhere to be found.

My plan was to introduce him to Cooper as I knew the two would hit it off. I wasn't sure why Al hadn't called back, but I needed to make some progress.

"You guys okay over here?"

The waitress was an older lady who looked like she was losing the battle with aging. The wig she wore was lopsided, and her makeup looked stale.

"I'll take another Heineken," Cooper said, then he motioned to me. "You having another drink?"

That was code for me to say no. We were always on a tight budget. I didn't mind because when Big Al came in, I wanted to be sharp, so I could hammer down something tangible for Cooper. We needed the gig.

That night, Big Al was a no-show, and Cooper had not been impressed. It would be two more weeks after that, before I finally heard back from Big Al.

Yesterday and I were out at the mall when the call came in.

"Aey, this is Al," was all he said.

He behaved as if he hadn't seen a ton of missed calls from me. I hated when people ignored you for no reason at all, then circled back like nothing happened, and failed to even acknowledge your efforts to reach out. I wanted to scream at him and ask if this was how he conducted his business. But instead, I simply said, "How are you?"

"Can you come by the club?"

I wanted to ask why. I wanted to ask whether he had decided to let Coop sign. I wanted to ask or say a lot, but instead all I said was, "when?"

"Come in the next couple of hours. I'm headed that way soon."

Thoughts of how he kept me waiting the first time flashed through my mind, but still, I didn't complain. I felt like any cross word to him would taint his decision about Cooper, and I couldn't take that chance.

I hadn't developed a single lead in the time I waited to hear back from Al. Cooper still had no chance of landing a residency anywhere, and it was frustrating.

Cooper's impatience seemed to grow by the day. Nothing I was doing was fast or good enough as it related to his career. I couldn't tell him, but I never imagined it would be as hard as it was. Since I had no connections, and didn't know any of the right people, it felt like we were stuck.

"I'm out with a friend now," I said.

Yesterday looked at me with curiosity all over her face. But she didn't need to get the scoop until I was ready to give it.

"Come alone," was all he said before he hung up.

"Who was that?"

"This club owner who keeps stringing me along. I'm trying to get Cooper a weekly gig there, but he acts like he can't return a call."

"Umph, shiesty," Yesterday said.

Deep down, I knew she was right. All the signs pointed to a man who lacked professionalism, was probably shady beyond words and more than a little dangerous, but I needed his help.

"Listen, let me drop you at the nail shop, then swing by his place. By the time you're done, I'll be back to scoop you."

"You do get that we were supposed to be spending the day together, right?"

"I know, but I really need to get this gig for Cooper. He's already on my ass about the little family-reunion type stuff I've booked. I need something big, and this could be it."

Yesterday looked up one direction, then down the opposite as we stood outside of Victoria's Secret.

"Okay, let's go," she said.

She was cool to let me drop her off, so I could rush over and beg for work for Cooper. As I drove like a crook running from police, my mind raced with all the things I could say to try and nail down something solid from Al. I needed to get him to commit to something even if it was only a one-time performance.

This time when I pulled up outside the club, the scene was different. The parking lot looked deserted, and there was hardly anyone hanging around. Even the workers were scarce.

If music hadn't been blaring from the door that sat ajar, I would've expected to wait on Al again. But I knew he was inside.

When I walked in, it took my eyes some time to adjust to the sudden darkness. The cool air was refreshing, but the place smelled like stale liquor and cigar smoke.

"Hello, Al? You in here?" I called out.

I didn't want to surprise anyone, and I didn't need any surprises.

"Aey," he said as he stepped into the doorway of his office toward the back of the club.

The hallway looked darker than the rest of the building. Big Al pointed to his earpiece, indicating he was on the phone, then beckoned me toward the back with the wave of a hand.

"Yeah, Playboy, that sounds about right."

He pointed at the chair in front of his desk and I sat down. As he talked on the phone, I tried to think of exactly what I would say to convince him to let Cooper play his club. Suddenly, everything I had rehearsed in my head on the drive over was gone. I was nervous. He was important in the nightclub industry, and he could possibly lead me to other gigs for Cooper.

"Bet that," he said into the phone.

As he talked, his eyes seemed stuck on me. Being beneath his deep penetrating glare made me feel even more uncomfortable, but I wasn't about to back down. I was determined to leave there with some kind of commitment. It had taken too long to get him face to face. Since he rarely returned calls, I felt like I needed to make the most of the rare opportunity.

"Okay, well listen, dawg, I gotta go. I'm sitting here bullshitting with you, but a fine young thang is waiting on me, and I don't know how much longer she's gonna wait."

That description took me by complete surprise.

The fact that he said it in my presence left me baffled. I don't think anyone had ever referred to me as a "fine young thang." Suddenly, a different type of nervousness flooded my system, and I wasn't sure how to adjust.

Time wasn't on my side, either. Big Al ended his call, then leaned back in his large chair, and focused his razor-sharp stare on me.

"So, did you get a chance to listen to Cooper's demo?"

I nervously jumped right into business, thinking I could steer the conversation in the direction I wanted.

He didn't respond; he just continued to stare. I prayed that my nervousness wasn't as obvious as it felt. When the sweat rolled down the middle of my back, I wanted to throw in the towel, but I knew I couldn't.

Finally, he spoke, but it wasn't what I expected him to say.

"Come over on this side of the desk," he said. He patted a space close to him. I hesitated.

I swallowed dry, but I knew Al probably wasn't the type of man who waited long.

My legs felt unsteady as I stood. That might have been the first, but it certainly wasn't the last time I had to give something in order to make things happen for Cooper.

Chapter Twelve

I walked into the house, stripped naked, and headed straight for the shower. With the water as hot as I could stand it, I stood underneath a constant downpour that couldn't clean me no matter how long I stood there.

Those memories would never go down the drain. I closed my eyes, and it was like Big Al was touching me all over again.

"You like that?" he'd asked as he squeezed one of my nipples through my bra.

I didn't want to admit it, but it felt really good. My body responded to him before I could find my words. Our eyes had locked.

When I'd nodded, he'd pounced.

Big Al had pushed me back onto his desk, pulled up my blouse and hungrily attacked my nipples. At first, he had cupped my breast and suckled like it was filling his thirst. He had wet my skin, pulled back and allowed the air to hit it, driving me to the edge. I didn't want to like it, but my senses took over, and soon, there was so much heat and pleasure coming from his touch, I thought I might lose it and scream in ecstasy.

In the beginning, I had scolded myself for falling so easily, but the minute pleasure took over, it was like my morals and professional principles abandoned me.

When I'd tried to back up so that I could take the bra off, Al had stopped me.

"No, leave it on. Just hike up your skirt."

I felt like a horny teenager doing something wrong. He had cleared a little space on the desk, but for the most part, every time

I'd moved, something fell to the floor. Al wasn't the least bit bothered. He'd kept his eyes on me as his hands explored my body. He wasn't gentle, and I didn't mind. There was no love or warm feelings involved.

"Damn, you're so wet; that's what's up."

With two thick fingers, he'd fingered me for a few minutes, then dipped his head between my thighs and used his tongue to separate my lips. My body had pulsed with hunger as he'd touched me. The more he'd touched, the more I'd wanted. It was the most pleasurable tease I'd ever encountered.

"Shiiiit," I'd managed. I'd bit down on my lip to try and suppress what I'd wanted to say.

He'd spread my legs wider, licked and sucked me so hard, my panties that had been snatched to the side, kept slipping between his tongue and my swollen flesh. The sensation was amazing. I'd closed my eyes and allowed my mind to enjoy the pleasure my body enjoyed.

"Oh, my." I couldn't control it. I was being swept away, and I'd decided to let go.

Suddenly, everything had stopped. I'd opened my eyes to see him looking down at me.

"I wanna fuck you."

"I want you to," I'd admitted breathlessly. All shame had exited my body, and I was alone.

Big Al had unzipped his pants and allowed his massive dick to tumble out. My eyes had grown wide at the sight of his size.

"Whoa!" I'd licked my lips instinctively.

"Yeah, that's the reaction I get with this." He'd stroked himself and motioned for me to come closer. Mesmerized by the sheer size, I could hardly move.

"Don't be scared."

When I still didn't move, he'd come to me and all but stuffed himself into my mouth. It didn't take long for my jaws to ache, but Al was relentless. He'd held my head in place as his erection quickly filled my mouth.

He'd moved like he was trying to push out my tonsils, but I'd enjoyed it. I'd enjoyed the forbidden nature of what we were doing, and all that was wrong about it.

After a few near unbearable minutes, water had filled my eyes and I gagged. That's when he finally had stopped. Just as I thought I'd get a chance to catch my breath, Al had adjusted my body on the desk, and entered me with such force, it felt like my insides were on fire. But soon, the pain had danced with pleasure and sent my senses into a blissful state of euphoria.

"Hey, condom, you need a condom," I had cried.

I had believed he'd heard my voice, but he didn't respond and he wouldn't stop. He was in his own world. Al had released a groan as his hips gyrated, and every time he'd pushed, he'd pulled me closer. He'd felt like wet steel as he'd entered me and pulled out. He was hard and wet, and my body wanted more.

"Oh, God!"

He'd filled me.

"I'm Big Al, baby; I'm Big Al." He'd moved in sync with his words, "I'm Big Al."

"Felicia?" My mother's voice interrupted my thoughts of the best sex I had experienced in quite some time.

"Yeah?!" I yelled.

"Phone for you."

I rolled my eyes. Why was she announcing calls from my cell phone? Living with her helped us out, but she knew no boundaries. Most times my mother behaved as if we were still kids.

My sister and I were so eager to get away from home, I never thought I'd be back under her roof. Yet, there I was, struggling to make Cooper's dreams come true.

"I'm in the shower," I said.

"Yeah, you've been in there for almost an hour, but you got a call."

Now she had issues with the length of my shower. Reluctantly, I turned off the water, grabbed a towel, and covered my body. Before I could pull the curtain back completely, she stood there with the cell phone.

"Geesh! You scared me!"

"I don't see why. I was just talking to you."

"Yes, but I didn't say come in."

"Chile, please; this my house. I ain't gotta get permission to go anywhere in here." She shoved the phone toward me. "Here, this thing been going off like a slot machine!"

"Why'd you answer my phone?"

My mother looked at me like I was being ridiculous.

"Sweet Jesus! Didn't I just say it's been ringing like crazy?"

She didn't wait for an answer before she turned and walked away like she had done nothing wrong.

I was somewhat relieved when I noticed that she had muted the call.

"What took so long?" Big Al asked. He sounded angry.

"Oh, sorry, I was in the shower." Panic settled into my nervous system because a call from Big Al was all I'd been waiting on.

"We want your client for four weeks; at the end of that time, we can renegotiate."

I wanted to scream for joy as I listened to Al tell me about the terms of our agreement. The money wasn't what I expected, but Cooper would blow them away, and I planned to negotiate an increase once the gig was permanent.

"You cool?" he asked.

"Yeah, but I want to be clear. Is there a chance for a long-term agreement, or are we just filling in?"

"If, at the end of four weeks, both sides agree and want to continue, we can sit down with Lenny, the manager, and go over a detailed contract. Right now, let's start with every Friday for the next four weeks, cool?"

"That'll work. We'll see you Friday," I said.

"We'll see your client Friday, but I need to see you Thursday evening, at the club. And don't wear no panties."

Chapter Thirteen

My appetite was completely gone, replaced by the strong urge to bitch-slap Cooper right there in the middle of the restaurant. We had gone there to celebrate what should have been an incredible milestone in both our careers—his as a singer and mine as the manager. I was so filled with rage, and when my mother poked her nose into the conversation, it didn't help.

Initially, she was on my side, and shared in the excitement I tried to build around the announcement. But the minute Cooper threw his tantrum, her position changed faster than the temperature in Texas.

"Well, Felicia, hear him out. I think he's got a bit of a point," Tabitha said.

It was still hard for me to wrap my consciousness around Cooper's lackluster reaction to what should have been great news.

Sure, I could have simply told him back at the house when he'd walked in after work, that we had finally done it, that he finally had his very first weekly gig, but I wanted to make the moment memorable. I was proud of the accomplishment, despite what it had taken to close the deal.

The wait for Cooper to get home from work was almost unbearable. I was at the door the second he walked in.

"Babe! What took you so long? I've got great news. C'mon, change; get out of your uniform, and let's go out to eat. We're going out to celebrate."

Cooper's expression was one of confusion and surprise. He seemed a bit lost.

"Celebrate what?" Cooper asked.

"The great news; now hurry and go change!"

I tapped my wrist where a watch would have been, to emphasize his need to hurry. But he seemed to move even slower.

"You can just tell me now. I don't know if I feel up to going out."

His attitude would stink up the entire place if I allowed it to take over. Before I could respond, my mother came walking into the living room. She and Trey were dressed and ready to go.

"Cooper, c'mon now; some of us are hungry, and your wife not gon' let us eat until she shares the news. Hurry and go change; we ret' to go!" At times, my mother dealt with him the same way she dealt with our son. It was effective when she did it, but never worked for me.

Cooper tossed me a look I couldn't decipher, but he turned and walked toward our area of the house, without another word. A few minutes later, he returned dressed in dark jeans and a polo shirt. With very little effort, he always looked good. That's why I knew for sure he'd be perfect in a weekly gig. If he didn't have anything else, he had the look of a sex-symbol, and he knew it.

My mother rode in the front seat, Cooper drove, and I sat with my son in the back. On our way to Pappadeaux, Cooper and my mother talked about what they thought the news could be.

I intentionally ignored them because I wanted to unveil it in my own way.

Once Cooper parked, he jumped out, ran to the other side, and opened the door for my mother. I was furious. I sat there for a few minutes as they talked and wondered how long it would take for either to realize the baby and I were still in the car.

Cooper finally took the hint, and opened the door. It was the wrong side, but I had to settle for that.

The restaurant was abuzz with activity. Music from overhead speakers added to the backdrop of laughter and chatter. Then the aroma of various seafood dishes lingered in the air, and made my stomach do a somersault. I couldn't be sure if that was from the excitement about my news or hunger.

We were seated in the center of the restaurant, and the waiter had just taken our orders. After he left, I commanded everyone's attention and began.

"So, you guys know how hard we've been working to get a residency for Cooper, right?" I paused, and then looked around.

Everyone appeared anxious, on the edge of their chairs, as they hung on to each word that cautiously slipped from my lips.

"Damn, Licia, why you playing?" Cooper finally said.

My mother rolled her eyes as she tore off another piece of warm bread.

"She and Eve always played too much," she said, and then stuffed her mouth.

We hardly talked about my sister, and when my mother mentioned her, it was usually in connection with mischief or something negative.

"Okay, okay." I cleared my throat. But just as I was about to make the announcement, our waiter returned to refill water and tea glasses.

"Get real!" Cooper exclaimed.

I shrugged. "What? How's that my fault?" I motioned toward the full glass before I brought it to my lips and took a long and slow sip.

"Licia, quit playing and c'mon!" He huffed. "You don' dragged this out long enough. Spill it."

In an attempt at calming the nerves, I gestured with my hands to quiet them down.

"Okay, fine. You people don't know how to have fun."

With all eyes, including Trey's, on me, I sat upright in my chair and proudly announced, "You are now looking at the newest performer for Friday nights at Milan's of Houston!" I did jazz hands in Cooper's direction.

But Cooper's blank stare threatened to slice my heart into pieces. My mother's expression went from unimpressed to surprise, then glee.

She jumped up from her seat, rushed to the other side of the table, and pulled Cooper into a big hug. After covering the side of his face and head with congratulatory kisses, she came over and squeezed me.

Our son seemed excited although he probably didn't know what was going on.

My mother wouldn't stop. "You did good, baby, you did it!" she cried.

The fact that she sounded so surprised was a bit discouraging, but it was Cooper's reaction or lack of one that sent my blood boiling.

"That's what all this hoopla was about?" His expression twisted. "Isn't that place like a hole-in-the-wall?"

It felt like someone deliberately let all the air out of a big birthday balloon.

I felt my face fall at his reaction. But my mother continued on, she snapped her fingers and wiggled in her chair as if she were moving to music. "Baby, back in my day, before I found the Lord, some of the best times was had in those so-called holes-in-the-wall."

With all of the things she did to irritate me, I appreciated her effort to try and show Cooper the bright side of this situation.

"When we agreed to do this, I thought you were working on some real stuff, not just reaching for low-hanging fruit," he deadpanned.

At that moment, all I could think was how much I had sacrificed to get him the gig he didn't want.

"I ain't saying I'm not gonna do it; it's just I gotta think about other things like safety and shit like that, Licia. We're gonna be hanging around that area late at night on weekends. Shiiiid, anything could happen."

He knew pulling the safety card was a way to gain my mother's support. Just as quickly as she had celebrated my accomplishment, she was now uncertain after having heard Cooper's concerns.

They both made me want to get up and walk out.

"Besides," Cooper began. "I thought you was trying to get something started with the city."

I threw my hands up. "Yes. I am trying to get something started with the city, but do you think that happens overnight?"

"Not overnight, but at least let me know that you trying to get me the type of gigs that count. When you convinced me to do this, I didn't think you was thinking about these ghetto places. We better than that," he said. His sharp words had caused enough damage, but I still had to look at him shaking his head, and that made me wonder what the hell was rolling around in that blank mind of his.

As the waiter approached, I was relieved. When our food came, I figured that gave us all the chance to cool down. Since we didn't go out to eat often, when we did, it was usually a festive time— lots of laughter, jokes, and good chat. However, this meal could have easily been mistaken for the last before an execution.

Long faces crowded the table, and I had no desire to speak to either my mother or Cooper. Our son ate and played with his handheld game.

That was the beginning of a long, love-hate relationship between Cooper, Big Al, and me.

Chapter Fourteen

The sound of sirens pulled me back to the present. At first, I was nervous, thinking a situation had broken out, and Mr. Belton had called the law. But as quickly as the sound grew, I listened as it went from loud, to louder, then settled and became another distant sound.

I eased back and returned to the memory. In an instant, I was back in that restaurant, feelings and emotions on fire like the blaze had just been sparked.

I excused myself, got up, and said, "Going to the bathroom."

No one reacted as I left, and on my way toward the back of the restaurant, I saw our waiter. "Please take this card for the bill at that table."

It wasn't that I needed to go, but I needed a break from all of the misery at the *celebratory* dinner.

As I made my way to the bathroom, I thought about all I had sacrificed to make things happen for Cooper. He never appreciated anything I did for him; it was never enough. But I was part of the problem too. I let him get away with way too much shit.

While I was pissed at him, as I rushed into the bathroom, I was really upset with myself too. Thoughts of his other indiscretions came to mind.

One evening, I had to stop and literally beg God for strength. I wanted to approach Cooper and our gig with the best attitude possible. So in order to do that, I needed to pull myself together.

We were signed up for a gig that I had been happy to book.

One of the area fraternities needed a singer to accompany a string quartet. Cooper was a perfect match, and I figured it was just another gig to add to his portfolio.

"Coop, c'mon! You can't be late!" I was near the front door and was tired of waiting on him.

"Don't rush me, woman! I'm coming."

We weren't late, but when we'd arrived downtown at the swanky high-rise that housed a club on the top floor, the scene didn't match what I had in mind.

The party looked more like a frat house bash than a refined event for the grown and sexy.

I couldn't understand why a string quartet and a DJ would be playing the same gig, but as long as we got paid, I was determined not to cause any friction.

Cooper had looked around at all of the half-naked women who seemed to be competing in a twerking contest, then turned to me and asked, "You sure we in the right place?"

There was no way I was about to give the impression that I had made a mistake or didn't know what we'd signed up for, so I nodded and focused on the scene that played out in front of us.

"Well, I'm gonna move around a bit," Cooper had said.

"You're gonna leave me here alone?" I didn't mean for my voice to sound as panicked as it did, but that's the way the question came out.

"You scared some frat boys might try to holla?" Cooper had laughed at his own comment. I didn't find it funny at all, but I had stepped aside, so he could move around like he wanted.

He'd disappeared down the hall and into another section of the club. I couldn't help but wonder how I could have missed the type of event it was supposed to be.

Two girls had whisked by me, and nearly knocked me over. Neither had bothered to say "excuse me," but kept moving. I had stepped over to the side and somehow eased myself into a nearby corner.

As time had passed, the DJ had started playing some old school music that I enjoyed. A voice had sounded behind me. "You want a drink?"

I had looked around and thought, why not?

The man who had asked walked out from the shadows and came into view.

"What are you drinking?"

"Ah, I'll take a Vodka cranberry," I had said.

Why not? Cooper was off mingling, and I was alone, swaying to the music. I had wondered what time they would switch over to live music, but I was secretly enjoying the DJ.

Two drinks later, I had felt relaxed and ready to party. The man who had been kind enough to buy my drinks had moved on, but Cooper was nowhere in sight.

I had found my contact who had organized the gig—a short, round man dressed like a preppy model for Ralph Lauren—and had asked, "When are we switching to live music?"

He had looked around. "Well, I know I told you around ten, but the DJ is really hot right now, and as you can see, the dance floor is packed. Let me see what it's like in the other room, and I'll let you know."

Before he'd turned to leave, he'd looked at me. "No worries, though; y'all get paid regardless of whether or not you perform."

That had made me feel a whole lot better. However, I wasn't looking forward to explaining to Cooper why we still hadn't made it to the stage.

As my contact had walked off, I had decided to find my husband. He had no idea that we were being delayed, and he never even came to check in.

When I'd entered the other smaller room, I had noticed that dance floor was also packed. A crowd was forming around a couple who looked like they were doing one of those dance-off battles.

A sudden lump had formed in my throat at the thought that my old husband was probably putting on a show for these kids. Reluctantly, I had eased my way through the throng of people and made my way to the inner circle.

"Excuse me," I'd said. "Trying to get to my client,"

People were good about getting out of the way, but when I'd finally made it to the inner circle, I was relieved to see a woman and a man, who was not Cooper in the dance-off. I just knew he would be at the center of attention, trying to reclaim his younger days. I was grateful to be wrong.

Realizing Cooper was not where I thought he was, I'd decided to go in search of him before it was time for him to perform.

There were three other sections to the club. One housed an art gallery, where the artist discussed her works with party-goers, and the other held the buffet.

Cooper was nowhere in sight.

After a few minutes, I was tired of looking for a man who obviously didn't want to be found. Nearly two hours had passed since we'd arrived at this venue, and he'd never even bothered to check in with me.

I'd realized there was a terrace and decided to go grab some fresh air. My contact hadn't returned, and the DJ was still going strong. Once he'd confirmed we were still getting paid, I wasn't as pressed to locate Cooper.

A man had held the door open and I'd walked out into the darkness. The stars shone brightly, and it was a great night. Sections of the terrace were occupied by cigar smokers, and a few couples had the spots closest to the door.

Since I didn't like smoke, and I didn't want to see the couples with their PDA on full blast, I'd walked toward the back of the massive terrace. It wasn't until I'd approached the dark corner to the left that I saw the shadows. Alarm had settled into my brain quicker than a smoke detector invaded by smoke, and I was ready to tear up some shit.

"Coop? Is that you?" My heart knew it was him, but I had asked anyway. At the sound of my voice, figures had started to move in the dark.

Someone had bolted up from a crouching position, and Cooper quickly had turned away and fumbled toward his crotch.

"Are you fucking kidding me?!" I had screamed.

"Licia, don't trip. Hold up; hold up," Cooper had said.

The mud-dog of a woman had scurried away like she knew she'd been caught doing something out of order. But my anger wasn't focused on her as much as it was on him, my damn husband, and ungrateful client.

"Damn, I can't take you no damn where! Like, are you serious with this shit? You can't keep it zipped while we're working!"

"Licia, not here. C'mon, you ain't gotta lose your lid out here; you know all eyes are looking this way."

As he'd spoken, he still had fumbled with his groin and tried to adjust his clothes.

"You know what, screw you!" I had stormed off and headed straight to the elevator.

Chapter Fifteen

That night, as I had taken the elevator down, my mind thought back to only days prior when Cooper had originally pissed me off. I had given up more than I cared to admit for his residency at Milan's, and he did nothing but tear down the place, and me. Despite his ungrateful behavior, I still had forgiven him and thought this gig before he started at the club would give us a chance to warm up and get ready to introduce his act at his new home.

Instead, he had pissed me off yet again. His careless behavior had taken me back to the level of anger I'd felt that night in the restaurant. I'd tried to calm myself in the bathroom, tried to make excuses for why he was so quick to criticize.

"You waiting to use it?" asked a woman who squirmed as she stood behind me.

I stepped to the side. "Oh, sorry; no, go ahead."

Her question brought me out of that memory. It didn't matter how long I stayed in the bathroom, Cooper would only come looking if he were ready to go. I could be in there the entire night; he wouldn't give a rat's ass.

Better yet, I could get flushed down the toilet, and he wouldn't be bothered. I stood off to the side as traffic came in and out of the bathroom. I wasn't sure how long I'd stay in there, but I felt if I went back to the table too soon, I might haul off and do something I'd regret. That was what Cooper did to me. He made me so angry at times that I had to coax myself into doing the right thing.

After a while, I pulled in a deep breath and walked over to the mirror. I gazed at my reflection and tried to use strategies to help me realize that I had put too much work into Cooper's career to give up. He was a challenge, but once I helped make him a success, life would be better for us all. I had to keep believing that.

Instead of leaning on the many strategies I often used, I thought back to another one of his indiscretions. It was moving day, and I was so excited that we were finally about to leave Tabitha's house.

The apartment was nothing fancy. It was on the Southwest side, far enough away from my mother but still close enough so she could help with Trey.

"I need to run a quick errand and I'll be back," Cooper had said before he rushed out more than two hours earlier.

We didn't have much stuff to pack, so my concern was about the actual move itself, not the packing; it was just the principle of him leaving at that time.

After nearly three hours, I had called his cell phone. He didn't answer, so I hung up. The next time I'd called, when he didn't answer, I'd left a voicemail.

"Cooper, where are you? Can you at least call and let me know what's what?"

Another two hours had passed before I'd heard anything. And when I'd expected to see him after the door had creaked open, I'd looked up to see my mother.

"What's wrong with you?" I'd asked.

Her eyes had looked around the room. All of our stuff was packed up and ready to be moved. I knew despite how cramped we were, she probably didn't really want to see us leave. But nothing could prepare me for what she really wanted.

Tabitha had walked into the room and sat on the edge of the bed. By now, her back was to me, and that's when I had sensed her problem must have been epic.

I had walked around to face her and prayed I could avoid whatever drama was about to unfold. I was already trying to contain the rage that was building over Cooper being M-I-A.

My mother had looked up at me and her eyes were full. My heart had felt like it would burst from my chest.

"You know I am no saint," she had begun. I had frowned, because I had no idea where she was going with that.

"Before I got saved, I did some very unsavory things. God knows it is only by the love of Jesus' blood that I am still walking around here healthy, and alive, because if I was being judged today, umph, I'd be dead ten times over." She had thrown her hands up and cried toward the ceiling. "Jesus, thank you for your mercy, and all the blessings you have bestowed upon this family, even though we don't deserve it."

My heartbeat had taken off like we were the frontrunners in a competitive marathon.

"Mom, what's going on?" I had spoken softly. When she went off on her religious rants, I had to move lightly.

Her head had hung low and that really scared me. She was so hard to read.

"Baby, I need you to reach down as deep as you can and find it in your heart to forgive that man of yours."

Now I was really confused. I had no earthly clue what she was talking about. And what would she know about my need to forgive my husband?

"Forgive Coop? What for? You're scaring me; what's going on?"

By now, I was seated next to her on the bed. She had put her hand on my lap. "Men are different from us. They require extra care and attention. I know you are working your tail off to get this thing off the ground for your family, but, baby, a man can only handle so much rejection." My ears had started to ring.

"What are you talking about? Is something wrong with Cooper?"

"Baby, the reason he's not here is that he went to the doctor, and well, he got some bad news."

My heart had plummeted to the soles of my feet. What had the doctor told him? OhmyGod, cancer? Fear had crept up through my veins so quickly, I thought my mother might soon have to console me. But something else had hit me and I'd stopped.

"Wait, why wouldn't he tell me, so I could go to the doctor with him?" I had felt awful. He shouldn't have had to endure anything like a health scare alone. All of a sudden, the bad thoughts I had about Cooper weighed heavy on my conscience.

Suddenly, my mother's demeanor had changed. She'd cleared her voice and straightened her back. When she'd cleared her throat, I had braced myself for the bullshit.

"Well, now, it's nothing like that. I mean, he came to me first because he knows that I have a way of calming a situation before it gets out of hand." My mother could be just as self-absorbed as her son-in-law at times.

"What does that mean?"

My mother and Cooper were close, but I felt like any type of medical emergency should be shared between a couple before anyone else. This wasn't the best time to point this out, but I was bothered by it.

She had closed her eyes and exhaled. When she had opened her eyes and focused on me, she'd said, "Felicia, your husband tested positive for gonorrhea."

Blank stare.

My voice had left me and my head was threatening to explode. I had no idea how to respond to what she had just said.

"He did what?" I had stammered.

My mother's sympathetic tone and demeanor had vanished. Suddenly, she had switched to the no-nonsense voice of reason.

"Baby, men will do what men do. I'm just glad he felt comfortable enough to be up front about this."

My eyes had bugged wide. Did she just say he had been up front? How could a grown man go to his mother-in-law, of all people, and confess to contracting a sexually transmitted disease?

Then for my mother to even offer to act as a liaison to deliver this kind of foolishness like she was the mediator we needed made me sick. She had overstepped one too many times. Even if he had initiated such an awkward discussion, or even come to her out of desperation, she should have cut his ass off.

"So, my nasty-ass husband went out and screwed some equally nasty THOT, picked up a germ that he felt it best to tell you about first, his mother-in-law, versus his own damn wife whose health he put at risk by running up in some filthy trick unprotected?"

My mother's expression had looked as if she was exhausted with me! I had frowned and tried to find some understanding.

"See, this is why he came to me. I need you to calm down," my mother had said.

I had hopped up from the bed and rushed to my cell phone.

"You need me to calm down. My husband tells you that he has possibly infected me with some STD, and I'm the one who needs to be calm?"

"Felicia, we know you can take things completely left sometimes, so I felt honored that he felt comfortable enough to come to me in such a sensitive situation."

I had whipped around to face her again. "Do you hear yourself? He admitted that he has probably infected me with some germ, and you're sitting here trying to plead *his* case?"

She had used her hands to gesture and tell me, "I'm trying to have a civilized conversation with you about this sensitive situation."

Cooper sickened me. How could he be so stupid, and then share his stupidity with my mother?

"Mom, this is not about him overspending; this is not about the designer shoes he sneaks and buys when he knows we can't afford it. This is about something that could put my health at risk. I mean, if he must fuck around on me, the least he could do is use a damn condom!"

My mother had shaken her head. "Well, I am not gonna argue with that, but what I'm trying to tell you is, I've been there, and I've done it all. Honey, some men will just go with the flow and think later when it's too late. We, as the women and the superior beings, must rise above it all. I know that man loves you, and I know you love him. I'm sorry this happened, but it's the fact that he's trying to make it right. We gotta give him some credit for that."

I had pointed at my chest. "*We* don't have to do no such thing! I am pissed at his carelessness and his lack of discretion. I'm sick that he decided he'd take his chances with you instead of me… me, the very woman he has probably infected."

"Well, the reason he told me is because he knows that I will get you to go to the doctor, get checked out, and take the medicine you need to clear this up."

For a long time, I had looked at my mother and wondered whose side she was on. It seemed like she always took the side opposite of mine or me. What mother in her right mind would make it her business to endure such an embarrassing conversation with her son-in-law?

Sure, I had done things I wasn't proud of, but the things I did, I did for the betterment of our family. It was always all about him. Cooper did what made Cooper happy. He spent recklessly; he succumbed to lust; he'd probably steal if given the opportunity.

"How about, he should have told me?"

The ride home that night was silent for me. My mother and Cooper carried on in the front seat like I was not there, and it was okay by me.

As we arrived home, I received a message that changed the evening for me.

Chapter Sixteen

The sound of raindrops against the window pulled me back to the present. I was upset. Too much of my time and energy was being spent on a man who couldn't care less about me and my life. Sleep wouldn't come no matter how much I tried to focus on nothing. I closed my eyes, but instead of sleep at two in the morning, my mind raced with thoughts of that night I threw caution to the wind and thought of myself instead of Cooper for a change.

After the most miserable dinner we had experienced in a long while, I wanted to be with a man I thought could appreciate me and my hard work. So, I got things settled at the house, then turned to my ungrateful husband. "I have a meeting that could lead to something big for you."

Forget the fact that it was close to ten at night; I knew if Cooper thought he could get something out of it, I could walk out naked at two in the morning.

"How long you gonna be gone? Want me to wait up?"

"Nah, I'm not sure. I'm going to check out a potential venue, so I might be in late."

He had nodded, then pulled the headphones back over his ears. Since we'd been working together, Cooper spent most of his time listening to music. If he wasn't listening to some of his old performances, he was watching music videos of Usher, Trey Songz, and Chris Brown.

I had suggested that he fashion himself after artists like Brian McKnight, Maxwell, or even Tyrese. But that fool had looked at me and said, "I hope this is not a sign of how your hand is on the pulse of current music, because those fools are dinosaurs, and I ain't tryna compete with those old suckas."

The stare I'd given him was empty and blank.

"Whaaat, Licia? Ain't nobody checking for those dudes like that anymore." He'd smirked.

A common-sense suggestion suddenly had turned into an insult against me. Cooper had made me sick, but I told myself that was why I needed to go out and fuck Big Al until it hurt. And that was exactly what I intended to do.

I had responded to Big Al's text as soon as I decided what I was going to do, but still hadn't heard back from him. I'd told myself it didn't matter as I eased behind the wheel of the car and decided I'd drive to each of his clubs if I had to.

As I'd driven up to the club, my phone finally had chirped. I had pulled into a parking spot and picked it up.

"Really?!" I'd said as I looked down at the phone and saw the text message from Big Al. He had moved at his own pace for sure.

The message was an address. There was no other information; only an address in Sugar Land.

I had looked up at my rearview mirror and wondered whether I should turn around and go home. I shouldn't have reached out to him in the first place. Suddenly, a thought had clouded my mind. What if he took it out on Coop because I was a no-show? We needed things to run smoothly with this gig.

"Maybe I should just text back, and tell him don't worry about it," I had thought aloud. I had sighed.

Trying to figure out my best move, I had sat and thought about the pros and cons of going to see Big Al.

Nearly an hour later, I had pulled up at the address he had sent to my phone. Darkness had clouded my view of the house, but from the shadows, I could tell it was probably spectacular. Again, I had thought about going home, but then images of the last time Big Al was between my legs made me turn off the ignition. I had come this far; why turn around now?

I had pulled in a deep breath and opened the car door. In my mind, I had justified everything I was about to do. I had reminded myself of Cooper's selfish ways, his frequent indiscretions, and his lack of consideration for the sacrifice and hard work I put in. Images of his expressions during our celebratory dinner had fueled me to move forward. The initial guilt I'd felt after the first time I gave in to Big Al's advances had all but vanished.

The embarrassment I had felt at the frat party moved me to action with no remorse or regret. I had swung one leg out of the car and eased up from the driver's seat. My walk of shame along the pristine, shrub-lined walkway wasn't long enough for me to have second thoughts.

Before I had arrived at the door, Big Al had walked up from behind and said, "Hey, follow me."

As I had followed him toward the side of the house, it had seemed darker with each step. We had walked until we reached a cast-iron gate, where I stood back as Big Al had unlatched the gate and allowed me to step inside.

The oasis of his backyard was grand, even in low lighting.

"I was out here chilling when your text came through," he'd said.

The pool was small and intimate, and situated to the left of an elaborate outdoor kitchen, and a cabana that sat next to the Jacuzzi. There was a bottle of Hennessy with one glass next to it. *SportsCenter* was muted on the TV mounted above the stove. My eyes quickly had scanned his surroundings, and I was immediately jealous. But instantly, I had felt relaxed.

Big Al had taken my bag, placed it on a table, then said, "Take off your clothes."

He wasn't the least bit interested in what, if anything, I wanted to discuss. But the more I thought about it, the more I realized, when you got a late-night text from a married woman, I guess it was clear what she wanted. So there was no need for any kind of explanation.

Big Al had stepped out of his basketball shorts, eased back on the mattress in the cabana, and gestured for me to join him.

His erection was stiff and waiting. I had crawled up and used my tongue to lick up and down the length of his shaft. It had felt good against my tongue. He was such a big man—wide thighs, large hands, and a full round midsection. It was clear he ate and lived well.

"Lick the head," he had whimpered.

I had lathered him with my saliva and couldn't wait to feel him inside of me.

After a few minutes, he had moved me out of the way, reached over, and grabbed the largest condom packet I had ever seen. I was wet with anticipation. Any of the guilt I felt had vanished, and I was just hungry for him. One glance down, and it was very apparent that he was just as excited, if not more.

Once he'd slipped the condom on, he reached out for me to join him and I did.

Big Al had grabbed a remote, pressed a button, and the TV had gone off; it was instantly replaced with soft sexy music. The lyrics were explicit and that had driven me insane. I'd loved it. The surroundings, the music, and the sight of his erection had put me in the mood.

He had guided me on top of him and motioned for me to turn around. With my back to his face, I had lowered myself down onto his huge erection.

"Uh."

Once I had eased myself down, I gyrated my hips and moved slowly, savoring every inch as it slid in and out of me. Big Al had used his hands to slap both of my cheeks, gripped and held me in place. He had filled me in ways Cooper, or no other man, had.

"This is what you wanted, huh?" He had huffed as he worked his hips.

It didn't bother me in the least that he knew exactly why I had called, and he had no problems with it.

"Yes, Big Al, yes," I had cried.

I had bounced up and down with sheer pleasure. My body had released so much pent-up frustration. And I was thrilled to let it all go. Big Al had handled my body with such force I'd felt violated and good at the same time.

He had flipped me over and hovered over me, and I'd loved it. Big Al didn't put all of his weight on me, but he knew exactly what I needed.

He had pulled me closer and held me so tightly I had to tell myself not to catch feelings for a man who used sex to conduct business. There was no need to blur the lines. He only offered sex on his terms and nothing else. It wasn't his fault there was a void in my marriage, and he wasn't trying to fill it, either.

The slapping sounds our bodies had made as we connected were almost hypnotizing. And it had worked like an aphrodisiac for me. In that moment, it didn't matter to me what we were to each other; I just knew he helped my body release the stress that seemed to build up when it came to dealing with the lack of progress with Cooper's career, and Cooper himself.

When I had stared into Big Al's eyes and seen the same type of intensity I had felt, he'd exploded, and I'd come immediately after. We had breathed hard as he'd collapsed and nearly smothered me.

"Jesus!" I had cried. He'd jumped up, still breathing hard.

"You were good," he'd managed.

He made me feel good, not just physically, but good about myself. Cooper no longer cared about how I felt, and that had been obvious for years. Maybe it was because this thing with Al was new and felt exciting, but doing it made me feel vibrant and most important, desired. It didn't matter that what I was doing was wrong; it felt good, and after the disastrous evening with my husband, I needed to be around someone who understood appreciation.

"So listen here, we got this special gig coming up; yo client would be a good fit. It's at one of them fancy private events, but could be some good exposure, and it pays well too," he had added.

I had exhaled. I was still riding high after the much-needed, earth-shattering orgasm. But when I had caught my breath and processed his words, I had felt even better. I could appreciate a man who fucked me well, but when he looked out for me too, that gave me a mental orgasm which lasted longer than anything physical.

"Hell, yeah, just give me the dets, and I'm on it."

"Oh, he's gonna need a white tux," Big Al had said. "Men's Wearhouse."

In my head, I had started to think about how much it would cost to rent the tux. It didn't matter. If it were a fancy gig, I was certain we'd make back whatever we spent. And if we pulled it off, it might encourage Big Al to send more work our way.

A few minutes after we had confirmed Cooper for the gig, Big Al had rolled over, found his shorts, and slipped them on. I had lingered on the bed for a while until I'd realized he was waiting for me to get up.

A little bit of embarrassment had washed over me as it became painfully apparent that I had pulled a serious faux pas by having to take obvious hints that after a hookup, there was no need to linger.

Chapter Seventeen

Two weeks after my last tryst with Big Al, I was picking up Cooper's tux from Men's Wearhouse. It took forever for me to get him to go in for a fitting. Then, when I explained to him the significance of the gig, he tried to act like he wasn't impressed. Dealing with him was exhausting.

"Who is this dude anyway?" Cooper asked. He seemed insulted, and I had no idea why he would be.

His constant complaints were not the only problem, but the frowns and sour expressions that invaded his face with the damn complaints and threatened to push me over the edge.

If he cared about anything or anyone but himself, he'd be able to tell when I was frustrated, and maybe he'd try to curb his arrogance a bit.

"I told you he's the founder of the city's largest furniture store. He's well respected, and his daughter's wedding is supposed to be packed with the Who's Who of Houston."

Cooper rolled his eyes.

"So this dude made a fortune selling furniture. And now he's throwing some big-time party, and we're supposed to be what—the hired help?"

He frowned although there was no reason for him to have a problem with a high-profile paying gig, but of course he did.

Sometimes, the things he said really made me wonder about whether he suffered from a type of mental imbalance. Cooper complained when I didn't find him work, but when I found work, he wanted to scrutinize it. These were the times I wish I had a roster of clients. Cooper would find himself on the bench, and maybe that would fix his attitude. For the time being, there was no way I could consider handling anyone else, but it was something I planned to explore once I'd mastered Cooper's career.

"Coop, this one gig alone will pay several thousand dollars. I need you to show up, stick to the musical list I gave you last week, and go thrill these people."

He listened and at first didn't have a comeback, which was unusual. I braced myself. I knew him, and it wasn't like him to not find fault.

"Then that band, what's up with them? I see why they stuck doing the corny-ass wedding circuit," Cooper complained.

That was when I'd had enough.

I released a sigh. "Let me call and tell them, thanks but no thanks."

Cooper huffed. "Why you going there?"

The frown was frozen in place when I glanced at him. But something unexpected happened. Suddenly, his demeanor softened a bit, and his expression returned to normal. He looked at me like he wanted to test me and see whether I would retreat.

"I work hard to find good work for you, and all you do is complain. I get tired of it, Coop. You don't know what all I do to get you a gig. It's not as easy as telling someone that you have a great voice; there are lots of singers with great voices. I need you to act like you have some damn appreciation for what I do."

"C'mon, Licia, you know I 'preciate everything you do. But I gotta be able to tell you how I feel about stuff, so you'll know how I like to move around." He eased closer to me. It wasn't an apology, but it was probably the best I'd be able to get from Cooper. He looked so good and refined in his tux, it wasn't easy to stay mad at him.

There was nothing better than a man dressed in a tuxedo, so

when he came up on me, and used those powerful eyes to pull me in, it was me, and not him, who softened. Cooper was already a handsome man, but dressed and polished in that tux, he looked irresistible, like God made him to tempt.

"Why I gotta gas you up just so you know I appreciate what you do? We a team, right?"

I nodded, still memorized by his appearance.

We were a team, but each player needed to do their part, and that was the part Cooper failed to realize. He wanted everything the way he wanted it, and there was no room for compromise.

Accessories complete, dressed and ready to go, Cooper looked like he could grace the cover of any fashion magazine, and he knew it. He started posing and profiling, and that instantly lightened the mood.

"Ya man clean up nice, huh, baby?" He tilted his head and used one hand to elevate his chin.

He did clean up real nice, but I wasn't about to give him that extra stroking he seemed so desperate to get. I brushed off his antics.

"Let's go before we're late. The band wants to do a sound check," I said.

As we walked out to the car, and at the sound of that, Cooper paused and huffed. "Damn, this is the most practicing band I've ever worked with. The list ain't even hard; they just a bunch of corny-ass dudes." He shook his head as he opened his door and climbed into the car. I stood for a few minutes and tried to calm myself.

After a mental count to ten, I pulled in a breath, opened the car door and slid in behind the wheel. It was all I could do to drive in silence as he continued to complain about each and every musician in the band.

As I pulled up to the light at the corner, my eyes fell to the gas tank. That's when I noticed the needle was below *E*.

"Shit! We need gas," I said.

"Damn, Licia, I ain't got no money." He leaned in closer and looked over at the gas gauge, then flopped back on his seat.

"You don't even have five dollars? All the cards are maxed out."

Cooper threw his hands up. I was so frustrated. I wanted to tell him we'd have money for gas if he wasn't constantly shopping, but the money for the tux probably had pushed us over the top. However, I had to look at it as an investment; we needed the money the gig would generate.

"How far we gotta go?" Cooper leaned over and looked at the gas gauge again. "Shiiiid, we below empty."

"You don't have anything to contribute?" I couldn't take the attitude out of my tone. I was pissed.

"Nah, shit. I'm broke. What we gonna do?" Cooper looked at me like I was supposed to solve all of his problems, and I guess, as his manager, that was my job.

The gas gauge indicated we had fifteen miles' worth of gas. My mind went into overdrive. It sickened me to be so broke that we couldn't even buy gas.

"Here's what's about to happen. We're gonna go into the next gas station, and get some gas; there's no way we're gonna make it all the way across town on less than fifteen miles' worth of gas."

"So what you saying?" Cooper asked.

He turned to me with a worried expression.

"I'm saying we gotta do what we gotta do; this gig is important, and we desperately need to get there."

"Yeah, but…"

Before he could finish, I cut him off, "But nothing, we need gas now!"

For a change, he didn't have a comeback or a complaint. He simply eased down into his seat and looked on.

When we were what I thought was far enough away from the subdivision, I started to look for the ideal gas stations. Once I selected the perfect one—dark storefront, one clerk on duty who seemed more concerned about her smartphone than work—I was ready.

After I pulled up to the gas pump, Cooper looked at me. "I thought we were broke."

"We are, but we need to make it to the gig, and I don't have a better idea; do you?"

"So, what are we gonna do?"

There were three other cars gassing up, and people moved in and out of the storefront. I looked at Cooper. "We are about to get gas. Now, are you ready to do this?"

He nodded somberly. "Yeah, you want to go in or you want me to?"

"Um, you fill up, and when you're almost full, I'll get out and walk like I'm going in to pay; that's when I need you to pull around to the side, and I'll hop in the car, then peel out."

I pulled up to the pump and waited as Cooper climbed out of the car. There was no way I could let on about how nervous I was, but my heart raced as I kept an eye on Cooper for the signal. He pressed the buttons to say we'd pay inside versus at the pump. By the time he surpassed $47.89, my pulse felt like it might actually skip a beat.

Cooper filled up, then he looked toward the clerk. There were five people in line.

"I don't need to go in because she looks busy."

Cooper looked so nervous I was scared he'd piss his pants and screw up the tux. Once I climbed into the car, I rolled up the window, and we drove off.

When we were a safe distance away, Cooper looked at me. "This is some bullshit, Licia. I need to get my mind right; you need to drive."

I looked around, saw nothing that appeared alarming, and

jumped out of the car when Cooper pulled over. Nearly thirty minutes later, as I pulled up to the venue, I couldn't believe what I saw or heard.

"Is this where we are supposed to be?" Cooper glanced around and frowned. "I see what this is gonna be; these folks are just throwing money away. Who the hell would go all out like this just for a freakin' wedding?"

Ignoring him wasn't easy, but there was no way he could complain about the incredible venue, or so I thought. The curb appeal was gorgeous. A modern stucco mansion with massive pillars created a scene that would've made a perfect backdrop for any Kodak moment.

"Are you ready?" I asked.

He looked over at the venue again, then at me and huffed.

"Yeah, I guess so. But I'ma give these clowns twenty, maybe thirty minutes of my time. Then I'ma need a few drinks to get me right."

Now this was not the type of event where the help needed to be tipsy, but there was no point in trying to explain that to Cooper. I didn't have the patience, and he did whatever the hell he wanted anyway.

Chapter Eighteen

The gig turned out better than expected. By the end of the night, Cooper had made friends with the saxophone player and the base player in the band. They, along with everyone else, praised his work. He had outdone himself and that was a good thing. I always told Cooper he should try to socialize more with musicians. That type of friendship could lead to more work.

As the band members broke down their setup, and the caterer and decorator started organizing and gathering their equipment, I tried to fall back so that Coop could mingle. Even though I was tired, it was more important for him to make some professional friends, and I didn't want to hover around like a nagging helicopter.

The show was amazing and I was thrilled. In addition to the musicians, there were three background singers. I had to admit, Cooper might have had his issues, but once he hit that stage, and with those ladies as backup, they were all on fire.

Cooper did a rendition of Luther Vandross' *Here and Now*. It was so good, so sultry, that at one point in the song, the bride, groom, and all of the guests stopped dancing to stare at him and the band. The sight gave me chills.

I had passed out business cards to several people who were eager to learn about how to book Cooper and the band. Two of the background singers left immediately after their last set. But one was still lingering; she was waiting on the bass player.

"He's real good," she said, as she approached me. She was friendly and had a great voice too.

"I'm Sonya; I'm the alto. Cooper is a quick study and that voice…" She shook her head, as if the sound he made brought back joyous memories. I knew what she meant, but was so glad he had been on his best behavior and didn't show his ass like usual.

"Where does he play?" Sonya asked.

"I'm still working on that. You know live venues usually already have their band in place, and the band always has a lead singer."

"Yeah, we've been together for almost ten years. But I really like Cooper; he jelled well with us, and that's not always an easy thing to do."

I was thrilled to hear such great feedback about him. For a minute, I was concerned about how he would get along with the band.

Sonya looked around and moved closer to me. "You didn't hear this from me, but just watch him around Jimmy. I ain't saying nothing, and I ain't told Jimmy to his face, but he can be bad news."

I looked off into the distance, where I saw Cooper chopping it up with two members of the band.

"Which one is Jimmy?" I leaned over and asked Sonya.

"Sax." Sonya used her arms to mimic playing the instrument. "Why you think I wait around and make sure Kevin leaves with me. If you don't watch out, Jimmy will talk up some after-hours spot, then ain't no telling what will happen after that." Sonya raised her eyebrows at the last part of the comment. Shit, I already had my hands full with Cooper and the problems he was able to generate alone. I damn sure didn't need anyone new adding to it.

"An after-hours spot?" I looked at my watch. "It's damn near three now."

Sonya giggled a bit, then said, "Honey, please; the after-hours spots are popping right about now. Then they really turn up and go strong until eight or nine in the morning."

I glanced back at Cooper. He didn't look tired, and outside of loosening his bow tie and removing the jacket to the tux, he looked prime for whatever might be next. If only I could have gotten him away from Jimmy. We needed to head home, not go to a damn party.

"Girl, thanks for telling me. We need to get home. I ain't trying to make another stop, especially not to no damn after-hours spot."

Sonya leaned over to look past me and yelled, "Kev, c'mon, dammit. I'm tired!"

That's when Jimmy nudged Cooper, and the two of them laughed as Kevin reluctantly headed in our direction.

"Remember what I said," Sonya told me as she and her man walked away and toward the exit.

"Say, Licia, why don't you go on to the house? I'ma go ride with Jimmy here to this little after-party."

I didn't want to blow Cooper up in front of his new friend, but Jimmy looked like he was higher than the clouds. He was rail thin, and had probably smoked an entire pack of cigarettes since we'd first seen him earlier in the night. When I noticed his black fingernails, I was disgusted. There was no way Cooper was going to leave alone with someone like that.

Cooper looked at me like he couldn't understand why I was still standing there.

"Not tonight, babe," I said. I tried my best to sound as tired as possible.

Jimmy's pierced eyebrow went up, as he continued to gnaw on the cigarette that dangled from the corner of his lips.

Cooper's head snapped back a bit. He flung his jacket over his shoulder and looked at me like he didn't understand what I'd said.

"C'mon, let's call it a night. You were incredible up there, by the way," I said as I tried to guide him toward the door. Cooper pulled beyond my grasp and shrugged me off. His actions were so rough and uncaring, I was embarrassed.

Jimmy lingered as if he were trying not to invade our privacy, but I noticed as he watched every move.

"I ain't hardly tired. Actually, it's the opposite; I'm kind of wired, so I'ma go hang for a little bit. Don't worry; I told Jimmy we rode together, so he's gonna drop me. You go on to the house and get some rest. I won't hang too long."

He must've thought I was crazy. I barely trusted him alone, but after all I had heard about Jimmy, there was no way in hell I was gonna sign off on that one at three in the morning. Oh, no.

"Can you give us a minute?" I turned and said to Jimmy. If he were smart, he would've picked up on my tone, which was intentionally harsh.

He looked at Cooper, then his eyes darted to me. "Oh, yeah, no prob. Coop, man, I'll be outside. I'm in the red Escalade sitting on those spinners."

What a loser! Jimmy looked every bit of sixty years old, and here he was bragging about some damn rims? No, Cooper would not be going any damn where with his ass. Now, I just needed to talk some sense into Cooper's simple behind.

"Why you trippin'?" Cooper asked the minute the door closed behind Jimmy, and we were alone.

"Trippin'? How am I trippin'? It's been a long night. Let's go home, make love, and go to sleep," I offered. My voice was calm, and my disposition was pleasant, despite the building frustration I felt.

"Last I checked, I'm a grown-ass man. If I tell you I'm going somewhere, I need you to say yes, and keep it moving. How you gon' embarrass me in front of my boy like that?" He sucked his teeth. "Besides, why you always gotta be on some kill-my-vibe type of shit! I just wanna go burn some of this energy; you knew I'm still on ten, and going to sleep ain't an option. And I already told my boy I was going."

"Coop," I began. I wanted to point out that that old rusty druggie was not his *boy*, but I knew not to say so.

"Coop my ass! I'm going, so this ain't up for no damn debate."

That's when I caught a whiff of whatever Cooper had been drinking. Then I realized I was dealing with tipsy, crazy-ass Cooper, and that was worse than any of his other personalities. This battle would be unwinnable.

I exhaled, fully committed to throwing in the towel at any moment.

"Lemme put the cheese on the cracker for yo ass!" he suddenly snapped. Pointing at his chest, he said, "I'm the man in this marriage and in this business. When I say I'm gonna do something, I'm gonna do it. I don't need your permission. Hell, I barely gotta tell you before I make my move."

Silence hung between us, before I retreated.

"Okay, Cooper, but I'm coming too. Tell Jimmy we will follow him to the spot."

Despite being the man he proclaimed to be, the minute I gave in, Cooper's eyes lit up like a child's. I was mad at myself for not putting up more of a fight, but I didn't have the energy.

We walked out of the building. I climbed into the driver's seat, and pulled out behind Jimmy's Escalade.

Chapter Nineteen

Knock! Knock!

My heart threatened to stop as the noise pulled me to the present. I never had company, especially in the wee hours of the morning. Was it Yesterday and my mother, still? I pulled the covers over my head and ignored the knocks and them.

It took no time to jump back to the past. At a time when I should have been rolling over after climbing back into bed following a late-night piss, I was squeezing past a throng of made-up, half-naked women who all smelled like alcohol instead of perfume. The music was too loud, the room was too dark, and I was too tired to be dealing with this shit.

The minute we arrived at the after-hours spot, a building that looked like an abandoned warehouse on the outskirts of downtown Houston, it felt like Cooper ditched me and vanished into the crowd. I was pissed, but I was determined to locate him and pull his ass out of there by his ear if I had to.

It was after five in the morning, and the party was still in full swing. The rooms were blanketed with dim-colored lighting, and people smoked, drank, and some dry-humped each other right out in the open.

This seemed to be an "anything goes" atmosphere where people came to let loose.

Once I made it out of the bathroom, I caught a glimpse of Jimmy hitched up in a semidark corner. He looked like he was barely hanging on. I shoved my way past a few people to get to him before I lost him too.

"Jimmy! Where's Coop?"

Jimmy's head seemed to dangle from side to side like one of those bobble-head dolls. There was a small trail of drool making its way down the side of his mouth, and I couldn't tell whether his eyes were open.

"Jimmy?" I reached over and shook him gently. The moment I let go, his body leaned to the side and slouched up against the wall. He looked like a rag doll with no bones. I looked around and not a single person seemed concerned about me, Jimmy, nor anything else. The music blared and people danced or made out where they were.

Unable to communicate with Jimmy, I left him and headed toward the back of the building. My senses were in a constant state of shock; if it wasn't the strong scent of liquor, it was the overpowering odor of weed lingering in the air. I was exhausted and ready to find Cooper, so we could go home.

Various rap songs battled each other by floating from one room to the next. Gangster rap blared through speakers in the main area.

Frustrated beyond belief, I began to open random doors and call out for Coop. "Cooper, you in here?"

"Knock, dammit!" a woman on her knees yelled.

"Sorry." I closed that door, then walked down the hall and opened another. "Cooper?"

This time a group of people were snorting coke, and I was sorry I ever interrupted. They barely moved as I opened the door, yelled, and looked around. He wasn't in there, either.

There was no way I could leave him there. Jimmy was in no condition to drive himself—much less someone else. And there was no telling what Cooper might get into if left alone. The more I thought about Jimmy, Sonya's words rang out in my head as anger mounted.

I should've taken my chances with a fight by telling Cooper we had to go home.

When I looked up, a few feet away, I saw Cooper hovering over a short woman. He damn near had her cornered, and I knew I needed to move in. I was happy and pissed at the same time. I was happy because we were finally gonna be able to leave, but pissed because from a distance, it looked like he was trying to mac on the woman. I wasn't in the mood for any bullshit, but I needed him to know that foolishness was not cool.

I marched up and snatched Cooper by his shoulder. "I've been searching for you for a while now, and you over here with some chick?"

"Aaah, Licia, my bad. This is the shit, right?" Cooper's words slurred, and he seemed unsteady as he stood.

"Who the hell is this?" I asked. The woman didn't say anything, but Cooper did.

"Who, Darlene?" He looked at the woman like she was a family friend who should've been known to me.

Short, plump, and half-naked, Darlene looked uncertain as she gazed back and forth between Cooper and me.

"Yeah, I'm Darlene, but all my friends just call me Dee." I wanted to tell Dee where she could go with her damn crusty lips, but going off on her wouldn't fix Cooper, so I didn't. There was no point in getting mad at Dee since it was obviously my husband who was all up in her face.

"Dee, I'm his wife, and we're about to go," I said.

She nodded, never reacted to the fact that Cooper was married, but said, "Okay then. It was good meeting you, Coop. Thanks for the drinks."

My blood boiled. Cooper had money to buy drinks for strangers but none for gas earlier, and hadn't thought about me since we'd arrived.

"Let's go!" I snapped. As he moved, I gave him a little shove the minute he stepped in front of me. I wanted to give him a quick kick to the ass, but there wasn't enough space to do so seamlessly.

Outside at the car, Cooper struggled to stand; he stumbled a bit, then caught himself.

"Don't worry; I ain't gonna drive," he said.

There was no point in responding, so I unlocked the doors, guided him to the passenger side, and shoved him inside once the doors were open.

Cooper was so drunk that once I buckled his seatbelt, he slumped over to the side, and I left him there. I felt like a misfit child who had broken curfew. There was no reason we needed to go to that after-hours spot.

Once I buckled my own seatbelt and took off, I was grateful that nothing had happened. I knew by the next afternoon when Cooper woke, he wouldn't remember any of this.

I made my way to I-10 when all of a sudden, bright strobe lights flooded the inside of the car. It wasn't safe for me to pull over right away, but the cruiser stayed close enough, so that I couldn't deny I was the target.

"Cooper!" I screamed. He didn't respond at first. I used my right elbow to jab him as hard as I could. The jab was extra hard for having us out late and for falling into a drunken stupor while I had to fight sleep to get us home safely.

He popped upright in his seat and quickly used his arm to block his eyes. "What the fuck is going on?"

"We're being pulled over."

"Oh shit! What'd you do? Damn, Licia," he growled at me, and looked over his shoulder. "Damn, you ain't drunk, are you?"

"Pull over now!" a loud voice from a bullhorn sounded.

"Shit! What you doin'? Pull this damn car over before they

think we trying to run, and shoot us dead." Cooper was wide awake and suddenly sober.

I eased the car to the shoulder and brought it to a stop. We sat there for what felt like it was close to forever. Cooper looked over his shoulder. "Licia. I know you're gonna be mad, but I gotta tell you something before the cop gets here."

My eyes were glued to the rearview mirror. I didn't need any problems. We were almost home.

"Look, Jimmy gave me some weed, and we didn't get to smoke it all, but I still got it," he said.

My nostrils flared as I released a heavy breath. What the hell was he thinking? He had random drug tests at work, and he was smoking with some druggie he'd just met?

"I think we should put it in your purse," Cooper quickly added.

"What! Why?"

"Licia, think about this; if they find it on me, a black man, I'm going to jail, no questions asked. You know that's not a good look for my career. But if they find it in your purse, they'll probably just give you a warning."

I had to think fast. What he'd said made sense. We didn't need him being arrested. He had to go to work Monday, but I also didn't want to go to jail, especially for something I didn't do. But I didn't have much time to decide. Reluctantly, I'd agreed, I'd say the weed was mine.

"C'mon, Licia. Here, let me get it before he comes." He dug into his pocket and pulled out the two marijuana cigarettes. "Where's your purse?"

Frantic and nervous, I looked around and tried to find my purse. I must've left it in the trunk. Damn!

"Here, dammit," Cooper said as he shoved the joints into my hand. I closed my hand and held my breath. By the time I looked to my left, the officer's face was inches from mine. I was sure he had seen everything. My heart threatened to stop.

"Ma'am, I need your license and your proof of insurance."

Instead of helping to find the insurance papers, Cooper leaned down, looked over me at the officer, and asked, "What did she do, officer?"

The moment I reached for the papers, one of the joints slipped from my hand. Unfortunately, I looked up and the officer's eyes were glued to me. There was no doubt he had seen the joint that had slipped from my hand. The officer stepped back, put his hand on his taser and said, "Ma'am, Sir, I need you both to step out of the vehicle."

"Oh, shit!" Cooper said.

Chapter Twenty

Hours later, I was booked into the city jail for possession of marijuana. What bothered me most was not that my husband drove my mother's car back home after I'd taken the rap for something he had done and probably explained to her, but it was the fact that he'd allowed it to go down the way it did. We'd agreed to do it, but that was when we thought I'd get off with a warning, not jail.

As the officer clasped the cold, hard handcuffs around my wrists, I noticed that Cooper didn't even wait for them to put me in the back of the cruiser.

He had already taken off. More often than not, Cooper showed me exactly who he really was, but there was something in me that refused to see what he showed.

I was slapped with probation for the weed, and given drug classes. But it was the ride home when my mother came to pick me up that was most painful.

"Now, I have done quite a bit in my younger days, but I ain't never dabbled in no drugs. When your husband told me what happened, I gotta admit, if he would've left, I wouldn't be surprised. Everybody knows, weed ain't nothing but a gateway to heavier drugs, and you know, I raised you and your sister better than that."

She was going in on me and didn't know half the facts.

"I'm just glad the folks at church don't know. We are living in trying times for sure," she said.

All I thought about was why my husband hadn't come to pick

me up. My mother might not have known exactly what had gone down and how it had gone down, but he did. It was clear that he simply threw me under a really low bus, and didn't even care.

"I don't know where I failed you. I pray for you each and every night and every morning; I don't know what else to do. I'm just glad you got yourself a good man who is sticking by your side."

If I'd had the energy, I would have told her about that so-called good man.

"Can you just get up off Cooper's tip for a few seconds?"

My mother pulled her eyes off the road to look at me.

"What did you just say to me?" She sounded so incredibly outdone.

"I don't know what he told you, but the weed wasn't even mine! Cooper's stupid behind met up with some druggie and accepted some weed; the two idiots didn't smoke it all, and that fool husband of mine decided to hang on to it. When the police came, he decided going to jail would be too much of a stain on his career, so I did what I always do: I took care of it."

The silence in the car seemed everlasting. My mother had no visible reaction to the news I'd just dropped, and she didn't say another word about the results of her parenting.

"I just want to put this entire incident behind me as soon as possible. Oh, but wait, I can't, because I now have to take some stupid drug classes, over some damn weed that wasn't even mine! I don't smoke, and I barely drink!"

Her head remained straight and she stayed focused on the road ahead. I was glad because I didn't want nor need to hear any more of her praises about my so-called good man. As she drove the rest of the way home, I made mental notes about things I needed to get done to make sure Coop's career was on the right track.

Later that night, as I walked into the bedroom, Cooper lay on top of the comforter, with his pajama bottoms on and his Beats headphones cupped over his ear.

He was grooving to some music with his eyes closed, and he barely noticed my entrance. When he did, he jumped up and snatched off the headphones.

"Hey, you're home," he said. Although he talked to me, his eyes kept dancing between me and his cell phone. There was no "thank you, baby, for what you did for me" or no "I appreciate you."

"Yeah, I'm home," I said. I was exhausted, both physically and mentally.

"Don't worry. I didn't tell Trey what happened."

My face fell, and I gave Cooper a blank stare.

Suddenly, thoughts of other things he had done, other things he had shared inappropriately with my mother, flooded my mind. I shook the thoughts off and continued into the bathroom. I wanted a long, hot bath and a new husband and client. But I knew at that time, the only thing I could control was the bath.

He followed me to the bathroom and lingered at the door.

"I'm working on a new song, an original. I think you're gonna like it." His enthusiasm defied logic.

What about me told him I was in the mood to talk or even think about his music. I had just come out of jail for some shit I didn't do, some shit he'd actually done. And he hadn't been the least bit concerned about my experience or what might happen to me because of it.

"Yeah, I let Moms hear it earlier, and she says it's fiyah!"

I struggled to suppress the eye roll I wanted to toss his way. I hoped my silence would be a hint to him that I was not in the mood to visit with him.

"I think I'm really on to something. You're gonna love it."

I turned the water on, dumped a cup of Epsom salt in the bath, and looked around for my favorite scented body wash.

"Yeah, when I make it big, and I know I will, I'm gonna take care of us. Like I already told Moms, I'm gonna hook her up too."

Sounds from the water filling the tub wasn't enough to shut him up, and that pissed me off. It was clear that Cooper knew if he kept talking, he could probably get me to forget about the real problem that was hanging heavy between us. That had always been his strategy.

"I'm gonna take this bath so I can try to relax," I said.

"Oh, yeah. You want me to go get the boom box, so I can play that new song for you? It might help you relax. It's real good, Licia."

I wanted to tell him the only thing that would relax me was if he were to go to bed and leave me alone. I wasn't in the mood to listen to Cooper talk or sing.

"I'm good. I just need to relax and clear my head."

"That's what I'm trying to tell you. This new song is live; all you gotta do is sit back, enjoy your bath, and listen as I serenade you."

"Coop, I need peace and quiet. I'm trying to think about some moves for your career, and right now, I need quiet to gather my thoughts."

"Oh, well, why didn't you say so from jump?"

That really was my bad because I should've known if he thought I was working for him, he'd do whatever I asked, so that I could focus. If I wanted peace and quiet for myself, that wasn't important, but if it was to focus on him, he'd make sure we could hear a rat piss on cotton.

Chapter Twenty-One

When I woke up, I felt completely tired. It was like I hadn't slept any the night before. If I wasn't in and out of memories from the past, I was wrestling with insomnia. Being single was worse on the weekends; loneliness clung like humidity on a Houston summer day. I wasn't sure exactly when Yesterday and my mother finally stopped bothering me, but by the time the sun peeked through my blinds Saturday morning, I felt more alone than I had in a very long time.

There was no hangover from my cocktail, but my heart felt heavy knowing my son had tried to call, and I didn't get to talk to him. If only I hadn't ignored the phone for fear it was Mom or Yesterday trying to call.

I dragged myself out of bed and nearly stumbled over my mother's designer shoes.

"Damn, these things." I snatched them up and put them in the corner near my bed. Who would pay a month's rent for a single pair of shoes? I knew Cooper had bought them for her, yet another thing to remind me that as I struggled, they lived a life of luxury.

"Maybe I should sell those bitches on eBay!" I laughed out loud at the idea of selling my mother's red bottoms.

As I made my way into the shower, I tried to come up with a plan to talk to my son. If I cleaned myself up and worked to keep my temper in check, things might be different this time.

Freshly showered and changed, I grabbed a yogurt from the refrigerator, used the Uber App to order a ride, and then enjoyed my breakfast as I waited patiently. In my mind, I went over all the reasons this was a great idea.

"Good morning, Felicia," the driver said as I eased into the backseat.

"Hi."

I put earbuds in so that he could see I wasn't in the mood for conversation. I tried to convince myself that this time would be different. I took it for granted that the phone call last night was to try and set up a visit. I hadn't seen my son in almost a year.

Evelyn and Cooper tried to act like they didn't stop Trey from reaching out to me, but we all knew the truth. As I sat thinking about the history between the four of us, it brought up deep-rooted rage that I couldn't seem to let go.

Seeing Trey after the breakup was more challenging than a boot camp program. There were times when we'd used my mother's house as a calm space, the neutral ground.

But it seemed like the minute Cooper and Evelyn realized what was going on, they started inviting my mother over to their fancy place for visits, which meant that my access to my own child was cut off.

One afternoon in particular, I wanted to see Trey, so I had asked my mother to offer to watch him.

"Well, if I do that, they're gonna tell me to come over there, and I'm not in that kind of mood," she had said. "Can you just call and see?" I hated to need anything from anyone, even my own mother. She only did things when she wanted; any other time wasn't convenient for her.

I had watched as my mother reluctantly picked up the phone and made the call.

Either she was just an actress by nature or she knew how to turn on the charm instantly. Her entire demeanor had changed immediately.

"Heeeey, Cooper, how's my favorite son-in-law?" My mother had cut her eyes at me after the greeting. She'd turned her back like that would plug my ears and prevent me from hearing her sweet-talk the man who had destroyed my life.

It didn't matter to me how she felt about him. I just wanted to see my son.

"Well, I was thinking you could drop Trey off and pick him up tomorrow? Miss Geraldine's grandkids are over, and you know they ain't seen Trey in a long while."

It killed me to have to resort to games and tricks to see my own child. But I had stood quietly and let my mother do her thing.

My mother had held the phone for the longest, without speaking, and it made me wonder what type of bullshit Cooper was spewing. But it was just like her to let him have his say.

"Uh-huh," she'd finally said, and nodded.

Her expression didn't reveal anything about the conversation, so I had no clue what was going on. Suddenly, she'd turned and leaned against the counter. "Okay, well, that does sounds like a much better plan. Okay then, I'll be here."

She had ended the call, then turned to me. "He says he'll bring the boy in a couple of hours."

I was relieved, but my mother had acted like she needed to say something, and I wasn't sure I wanted to hear it.

She had stood with her hands on her hips as if she were waiting for an invitation to speak her mind. I was trapped in a no-win position because she was bound to speak regardless of whether I wanted to listen.

"What's wrong?"

"How long do you expect to go on like this? When are you gonna try and work something out? God knows this ain't good for the boy."

"Do you not think I have tried? I just want to see Trey for a few hours." I had shaken my head. It wasn't the time to get into a deep discussion about Cooper and my relationship, but my mother did what she wanted like most people in my life.

"Well, I ain't one to be all up in your business, but to me, it seems like you'd wanna pull yourself together, if not for you, then for that boy of yours."

Being poor was not a condition that I could just snap out of, but people behaved like it was. Nearly a year after Cooper had left me, he was remarried, and on his way to living a dream life. I was broke, alone, and left to try and pick up the pieces.

He took my son for me and was able to keep him away just because I had no money. My mother always tried to act like she was a super Christian, but her role in the battle over Trey made her just like the devil. And I hated talking about it with her. It always turned into an indication that my life, not the way Cooper used his riches against me, was the problem.

The discussion about everything that was still wrong with my life was nothing new. Between my mother and Yesterday, I should have been real close to perfection. They were both pros at dissecting my life.

Nearly an hour later, it was showtime. I had found something to do in my mother's bathroom, so I wouldn't be detected.

"Mommmmy," Trey had squealed and jumped into my arms after the door closed behind him.

Of course I had to stay in the back room while my mother made small talk with Cooper. There were so many times I wanted to walk out and spit on that man, but that only would have made things more complicated.

"Hey, boy, soon I'm gonna have to look up just to look you in the eyes."

"I am getting taller, huh?"

Trey was eleven, and he was already the spitting image of a younger Cooper. He had his father's good looks, and I hoped my mild disposition.

That night, Mama had made tacos, and smoothies, we'd watched music videos, and Trey had attempted to show Mama and me the latest dances.

We probably appeared to be just another happy family, but there was so much turmoil and conflict in our lives, nothing could have been further from the truth.

Being around my son made me feel good, and despite his resemblance to his father, I loved our time together.

The ten o'clock news was about to come on when a knock had sounded at the door. It had pulled my attention away from the TV almost immediately.

"Who's knocking at your door this time of night?" I had given my mother a knowing glance.

She had quickly grabbed the lapels of her robe, pulled them together, and frowned as she looked around.

"I am a good Christian woman!" She had peeked her head around the corner as if she'd be able to see who was knocking. "I ain't got nobody calling on me this late at night."

"Well, are you gonna find out who it is, or what?"

My mother had gotten up and gone to the door. When she'd opened it, I'd nearly kicked myself for suggesting that she did.

Cooper had walked in and had come directly for me.

"We are trying to work with you, but when you pull this type of shit, it makes me feel like we can't trust you."

My son had looked bewildered.

"Trey, get your things and let's go," Cooper had said.

The boy had looked confused. When he'd turned to me, his

eyes were filled with tears. I could've killed Cooper. He didn't have to do any of that in front of my son, but he did.

"Do we have to do this right now?" I'd asked.

"Tabitha, you know we don't want to keep you from your grandson, but if you keep letting her use you like this, we're gonna have to change that."

"Cooper, the boy needs his Mama too," my mother had pleaded, her arms flared as she tried to make her point to no avail.

"If she wants to see her son, she needs to go back to court. We're not gonna keep going through this," Cooper had said.

What pissed me off most about this was that Cooper knew I couldn't afford a lawyer to fight him properly. But that wasn't all Cooper; it was really my evil sister pulling the strings.

I had been with Cooper long enough to know, if something didn't have a direct impact on him, he'd get bored with the battle and move on to something else.

But Evelyn, she was the complete opposite. She'd fight until her cold hands couldn't clutch anything else.

Chapter Twenty-Two

The Uber driver dropped me off exactly where I wanted. The neighborhood was quiet, with large colorful houses that seemed like the architects were all trying to outdo each other. From tree-lined streets to neatly manicured lawns, the area looked like someone took extra care when designing the master-planned community.

There were several cars parked around the cobblestone, circular driveway, so I knew for sure somebody was home. Actually, I noticed several cars; maybe they had company. I walked up to the fancy gate and let myself in.

At the front door, which was literally the biggest I'd ever seen in person, I pressed a button and waited for someone to answer. The elaborate doorbell could still be heard over the laughter and chatter bellowing from behind the door. So the Spears were having a party.

Seconds later, someone pulled the door open. "Oh, come on in."

When I took a step, my legs felt like they might give out on me at any moment. I had no business crossing that threshold, even if the person at the door were clueless. But once I was inside, it felt like I had slipped into a true oasis.

There were beautiful people gathered in a large open area only a few feet away. I couldn't miss them if I tried. Maybe it was because they had money or just looked like they did, but there was not a single ugly person in sight. Music played softly, and everyone held drinking glasses or plates of food. Cooper was having a party, so maybe he'd be in a festive mood. While the party explained the cars, the timing didn't make much sense to me.

It was obvious the person at the door didn't know who I was; I was sure Evelyn wouldn't have wanted me ruining her party.

I scanned the room quickly as I stepped inside. The TV cameras couldn't begin to capture all of the opulence that seemed to go on as far as eyes could see: the vaulted ceilings, custom drapery dressed windows that looked as tall as skyscrapers. The idea that Cooper had sold that many records didn't register with me.

As I looked around in awe, I didn't recognize any of the faces in the room, and it was obvious none of them recognized me.

For a few minutes, I walked around and looked at all of the fine furniture and expensive-looking knick-knacks that decorated the space. Everything looked nice, but it still confused me.

Who has a party in the middle of the morning? Man, Cooper really had changed. Was it even noon yet? Near the back wall of the large room, several chafing dishes were lined up on a long table. The table was stacked with silver flatware and matching plates.

"Do yourself a favor; you gotta try the Spanish eggs," a woman said as she whizzed past me, and darted to the table.

All of this was foreign to me. We never entertained like this, and not just for the obvious reasons, but I found it hard to believe that all of this fanciness was Cooper. It must've been Evelyn with her fake behind. She was always putting on a show and trying to make it look like she was better than everyone else.

I turned to go explore a little more, but bumped right into Cooper's chest, and froze in my tracks.

"Uh," I stammered, and took a few steps back. It wasn't as much fear as it was surprise. I swallowed hard and dry.

"What the fuck are you doing in here?" The vile words coming from his mouth were meant to sting, and it burned. He didn't even try to lower his voice. His face was twisted into a menacing scowl that threatened me with bodily harm. His eyes darted around the room, and I wasn't sure what that was about. My brain was trying to formulate some words that would explain the inexcusable.

"My son, he called me last night. I thought he needed me. I wanted to see him." My eyes followed his around the room. I still couldn't get used to seeing Cooper all dolled up and looking important. But even dressed up and with lots of money, he would always be the bitch nucca I knew he was.

"*My* son ain't here; he don't need a damn thing from you, and not only do you not have the right to show up here without calling, you know you're breaking the law," he said. The smirk on his face told me he intended to hurt me with that comment.

Around us, people stopped what they were doing, and all eyes trained on the brewing confrontation. I couldn't believe he was bringing attention to us in this way. Not only were people staring at us, but when they looked at me, it felt like they were judging me.

My clothes weren't designer, my hair and makeup hadn't been done in years, and that never bothered me before, but at that moment, I felt awkward and out of place. Even the hired help looked better than me.

As if the embarrassing confrontation between Cooper and me wasn't enough, Evelyn sashayed up to his side, crystal flute in hand. "Don't worry, baby; I've already called the police. I told you a long time ago, we should've pressed charges on her ass. If we had, bet she wouldn't be showing up like she owns the place."

She sipped from her glass and looked down her nose at me. I wondered whether that was the nose she was born with, but knew nothing that narrow could be traced to anyone in our family.

The next time their massive front door opened, two uniformed officers walked in. It was just like Evelyn to make sure she created a scene.

"She's right over here, officers!" Evelyn yelled. As if I weren't already the lone standout, the bitch had the nerve to point at me with her glass.

The officers approached. "Mrs. Spears, Ma'am, why are you here?"

"She's *Miss* Spears. Bitch still won't change her name years after the divorce," Evelyn interjected.

Cooper cut his eyes at her.

"I was trying to see my son," I said, ignoring Evelyn.

At the sound of my explanation, Cooper frowned and acted like it didn't make sense. He blew out a breath and shifted his weight to one side.

Suddenly, my mother, of all people, pushed through a crowd that had gathered to watch the impromptu show. The only thing missing from the scene was her falling to her knees and begging God to take her immediately, if he wasn't going to answer her prayers to "fix" me and my life.

"Felicia, chile, what are you doing here?" Her voice was laced with concern. "Good Lord, sweet baby Jesus, have mercy!"

"I don't know what she was thinking, but I'm sure she hasn't forgotten about the restraining order." Evelyn snickered. She made sure to enunciate every syllable when she mentioned the order. "And in case she did, I called the police just to make sure and jog her memory."

Evelyn turned to Cooper. "Let's hope this time, he's man enough to pull the trigger. You see how hardheaded she is!"

She used the flute to motion in my direction again.

My mother whipped around to face Evelyn. "Eve, you called the police on your own damn sister?"

Chapter Twenty-Three

My mother must've called Yesterday and told her that I was in jail. Three days after I was arrested at Cooper's house, Yesterday was my first and only visitor. I had gone to jail for Cooper in the past, but now, he was that same man who cheered when the judge ordered me to jail.

There was no honor associated with this latest arrest, and Yesterday knew that. There were times when I wished she would mind her own damn business. The last place I needed a visitor was in jail, but there she was.

"Felicia Spears!"

When the jailer called my name, I started to ignore him. I figured he must've called my name by mistake. Lying on that filthy cot, in that crowded, stinky cell, drove home the reality that I really had no one. Not that bail money was an option, but I had no one to call to even try and scrape up the cash.

"If she don't want her visit, I'll take it," another inmate said.

Two other inmates slapped high-fives and cracked up with laughter, as I pulled myself up from the thin mattress. The way the women's eyes began at my feet, then rolled up the length of my body as I got up, was telling.

Women behind bars had nothing better to do than try to get some shit started. I hated being in jail, even though on the outside, I'd been in a prison for what felt like years since Cooper turned my life upside down.

I walked out of the cell and followed the jailer down the hall toward the visiting room.

"Next time you hear your fucking name, you need to move like fire is under your ass!" he growled at me.

I ignored him, and kept walking. Once the main door to the visiting area opened, I took a deep breath. From across the room, as our eyes connected, Yesterday shook her head like she felt sorry for me. I didn't need her pity.

When I sat down, she exhaled. "You can't keep going on like this," Yesterday said. "Why'd you go over there?"

Her words were laced with pity.

"Trey tried to call the night before, and I missed his call." I glanced away. "I thought it might be you or my mother, so I ignored the phone. But I just wanted him to know that I wasn't ignoring him. Besides, I wanted to see him."

"But the restraining order," she whispered. "You gotta think before you do these things."

As much as I appreciated that she came to see me, what I didn't like was how she and my mother contributed to my misery, pushed me to the edge. Then when I went over, they wanted to behave as if they were so concerned.

"It was stupid of me to go over there, but I don't know." I shrugged.

"I know you don't want to hear this, but I've really been thinking about your situation, and I'm telling you, Felicia, I think you should consider doing some interviews."

She looked at me like she was trying to gauge my reaction before she went all in on the idea.

"Look, Yesterday, I am sitting in a full, nasty, stanky jail cell. Interviews are the last thing on my mind right now."

"Felicia. This is the second time you violated this restraining order. I'm sure that the judge will probably want you to sit in jail for a while this time."

My heart sank at the sound of those words.

Until she said it, I hadn't considered the idea of me possibly staying in jail. As crazy as it sounded, I felt like once a judge, or anyone, heard my side, maybe they'd understand. It didn't seem fair that Cooper was able to live this incredible life that I had worked hard to help him attain, without me. Who wouldn't be bitter after that?

"You've gotta move on with your life, sweetie."

I leaned forward, and that caused Yesterday to do the same.

"Move on, huh? How do you suggest I do that? You and my mother act like it's so damn easy. You guys expect me to move on like my own damn sister isn't married to my ex. Oh, yeah, and my damn ex is living the good life, that I created for him. Let me guess; go out with the mud-duck at work or anyone else for that matter?"

Yesterday pulled back and started to slowly shake her head.

"That's not what I'm saying, and I feel you, I really do. You're right; the fact that Cooper is making boss moves now; that's a bunch of bullshit. But, Felicia, what do you want to do about it? You can sit here and continue to follow down this destructive path or you could try and get some damn revenge."

Revenge?

She had my attention. I focused on her words like never before. I could use some revenge against Cooper and Eve. For years, the only things that came to mind seemed impossible.

"Think about it. Women love Coop; they love him because all they know is the story that he and Evelyn have put out there. Evelyn has worked hard to craft a brand that resonates with women. Houston native son makes it big and refuses to leave the South for the glimmer and glitz of fake L.A. He's right here to show other men what they should be saying to all these desperate, single, Southern women. Who wouldn't fall in love with that story?"

Her point was a good one. When Cooper had left me the way he did, I was ashamed. I felt like it was my fault, so I focused on my pain and misery. Fighting didn't even cross my mind. How would I fight? He had money but still took everything—my child, my dignity. I couldn't seem to get past the depression that set in.

Sheepishly, I looked up at Yesterday; until now, I had never thought about it like that. His story, the very one I helped create, was a real good one that tugged at your heart. Most men run to L.A. despite the stereotype of fake women, but Cooper's songs talk about the down-home Southern Belles in us all. His lyrics are made up of words we all want to hear.

"Yeah, people don't know the real Cooper," I admitted.

"But imagine if they did. Imagine if they heard all that he and your own damn sister put you through. Instead of being the victim, why not tell your side of the story?" Yesterday was working hard to convince me that I hadn't lost all of my power.

Using my hands, I dry-rubbed my face and released a hefty breath. What she said sounded good, but I knew for sure it wouldn't be that easy.

"You think people would care about my side?"

For years, I figured people only cared about him because he was a celebrity. America is obsessed with celebrities, and I thought even if they knew what he had done, it wouldn't matter much.

Yesterday's eyes grew wide in exaggeration. She pursed her lips and adjusted her body in her seat.

"I hate to put it like this, but real talk, he's so hot right now, they'll care about anything remotely related to him—truth, lie, or not. You have a whole lot more power than you realize!"

Despite myself, I was starting to get excited about what she was saying. Would the world be so quick to melt at his sexually suggestive lyrics if they knew that deep down, he was completely heartless? Regardless of how desperate women may be for a man, few would tolerate a man who mistreats women.

"And let's not even get started on his constant attempts to keep you away from Trey. Girl, please. I don't know why you didn't entertain this before. I kept telling you."

And she had. Yesterday couldn't understand why I never wanted to tell my side of the story. But the more I thought about it, the more I realized that in my attempt to let the truth be known about Cooper, it would have potentially brought out a whole lot of my own dirt. And that couldn't have been good for my credibility.

I wasn't sure if I were ready to air my own dirty laundry. I knew for sure, my stains were the kind that could really stink up the place.

Chapter Twenty-Four

Back in my cell after the visit with Yesterday, I thought hard about her suggestion. How much would I tell? What about the things I had done? How could I call myself spilling the tea about Cooper, when some of the shit I had done was hard for me to even think about.

I closed my eyes and tried to stop the tears that had threatened to push through. But all that did was cause more miserable memories to flood my mind.

Six months after we'd agreed to a residency gig at Milan's of Houston, I walked into a heated argument between Cooper and Big Al's manager, Lenny Brown.

Lenny was a petite man who got along with everyone. Despite his always sunny disposition, somehow, he seemed to rub Cooper the wrong way, and that always meant trouble.

"You need to deal with your client 'cause he on some ol' bullshit right now," Lenny said.

In the months we'd been at the club, I had never heard Lenny raise his voice. He was old school, hardly cursed in a woman's presence, but now, his eyes had transformed to slits, and he was breathing fire.

"Lenny, Lenny, let me handle this. I'll talk to him, just give me a few minutes." I tried to use my body as a barrier between Lenny and Cooper, and spoke as calmly as possible. But Cooper wouldn't shut the hell up.

"Fuck this shit! They expect me to do all kinds of shit for the peanuts they paying us; fuck 'em and fuck they damn contract!" Cooper spat.

I turned to Cooper, and through tight lips, I said, "Shut the hell up now, and allow me to handle this." If he didn't get it, my tone should've indicated that the situation was ripe, and he needed to back down.

"See, that's the shit I'm talking about. He's one ungrateful bastard! You know how many people who'd love to take your spot?" Lenny yelled.

"Let 'em have it! I don't need this shit!" Cooper huffed.

But he was wrong and he knew it; we needed the gig, and we needed it badly.

Unable to get through to Cooper, I whipped around to face Lenny. "Don't listen to him; let me talk to him alone. I'm sorry about all of this." I was desperate. "If I can just get him alone for a few minutes, I can help straighten this out."

In the time we'd been at the club, I wasn't able to make anything else happen for Cooper's career. The challenges were far harder than I'd expected. Everything was a struggle, and it didn't help that Cooper behaved like he had already arrived, and the rest of us needed to get with it.

With one hand shoving Cooper away from Lenny, and my other hand blocking Lenny, I was utterly exhausted with Cooper.

I turned to him and yelled, "Shut the fuck up!"

"I'm outta here. We ain't gotta do another fucking show!"

"You walk out, and we will sue your bitch ass!" Lenny barked back.

That was why I needed him to shut up. We were under a two-year contract with them, but yet, there Cooper was threatening to walk out. He had no damn clue about what it took to hold shit together.

"Lenny, please, just give me a few minutes, and I swear, I'll come talk to you. But let me get my client under control."

The deadly expressions the two exchanged made me wonder

whether I'd make it out of there alive. But soon, Lenny, released a heavy breath, looked at me and said, "You could do better than his bitch ass. I'll be in the back office when you ready, Felicia."

Before he left, he shot Cooper one last look and it wasn't meant to be friendly.

"Who the fuck you callin' a bitch?" Cooper screamed at Lenny's back as he walked out of the dressing room. I rolled my eyes. The minute the door closed behind Lenny, I lit into Cooper.

"Listen, I get it, this is not a fancy Vegas residency, but damn, Coop, do you really have to go on like this?"

He was looking at himself in the mirror. Although he tried to act like he was ignoring me, I knew he heard what I was saying, and deep down inside, he knew I was right.

"You can't get bent out of shape because the manager wants you to do requests."

Cooper whipped around to face me. "I ain't signed up to be signing no damn Happy Birthday to a bunch of wrinkled-up hoochie mamas. What kind of gig is this, and how long do I have to wait for you to make something real happen?"

"Coop, this is something real! Every Friday night, you're singing, what you love to do. It may not be much to you, but it is something. And how are you gonna get mad because club customers want you to sing something. That's what you're supposed to do; you're a friggin' singer!"

It took everything in me to refrain from violence. I wanted to literally smack some sense into him. He didn't understand what it took to get him a gig, and he had one, but would risk losing it over trivial bullshit.

"I'm better than this dump," he looked around, "and if this the best you can do, maybe I need to start looking for new representation."

At least three times a week, that was how often Cooper threatened to replace me. I was sick of it, but for now, I needed him to pull it together and do what the hell he was being paid to do, which was sing.

"I ain't fucking singing Happy Birthday tonight, so you need to go do whatever the hell you need to make Lenny understand."

Cooper turned away from me and put the earbuds back in his ears. Soon, he was stroking an imaginary air guitar as if I weren't still standing there.

There was nothing I could do to change his mind and convince him that sometimes we had to do what needed to be done to get along. But that would've been a waste on him. Cooper only saw things his way, and there was never any compromise. I rolled my eyes hard out of frustration.

Before stepping back out into the club, I took a deep breath and told myself this was all a part of management. Cooper was difficult, but I needed to overlook that and get the job done.

Unfortunately for me, the minute I walked out the door, Lenny was there.

"What's with him?" He nodded toward the door.

It pained me to have to talk nicely about Cooper when I was still pissed at him. But I couldn't avoid it because it was clear Lenny waited for me.

"You need to get rid of him, before he drags you down. I'm serious; it's like he walks around here acting like we should be glad his ass is here."

Lenny and the rest of the bar staff didn't know Cooper was my husband. We decided it was better if we kept our relationship professional.

Cooper thought people wouldn't take us seriously if they knew we were a wife and husband team. I didn't completely agree, but it wasn't worth a fight, so I went along.

Lenny wanted to stand and talk, but I needed to try and move him away from the door. Everything he said about Cooper was probably true, but no amount of conversation about it or him would fix all that was wrong with Cooper, so I took a few steps forward in hopes that Lenny would follow.

"You know I've got Big Al's ear, right?"

That question made my heart threaten to quit. Was he trying to say I'd have to get on my knees or my back to help the relationship between him and Cooper? I was getting tired of being the only person who had to put out to get something for an ungrateful client.

Before Lenny could clarify what he meant, the door swung open and Cooper stepped out.

"What the hell you still talking to him for?" he asked.

Chapter Twenty-Five

"Scooch down a little," a woman said.

Her order brought me back from that memory with even more rage in my heart. As I sat on a bench in a hallway, linked by handcuffs to eight other women down at the Harris County Criminal Justice Center on Franklin Street in downtown, my nerves were fried. One week after my arrest, I was still in jail. I wanted the mess to be over. I only had a public defender, and that meant my ass was as good as gone, but there was nothing I could do.

Everyone seemed lost in their own thoughts.

It was interesting to me that on a normal day, these were the same women who bullied, took part in catcalls, and ganged up on the weak, but today, they were all quiet angels as we waited to see the judge.

The door that led to the courtroom would open, one of the bailiffs shouted a name, an officer unlocked the cuffs to free a suspect, and she was escorted into the courtroom to face the judge.

It was so quiet as we waited, that I heard stomachs growl and rumble. My thoughts were also focused on what might happen to me. Seconds later, the door creaked open, and it seemed like everything fell to a slow motion.

Even the bailiff's voice took on an underwater-type sound when he said, "Felicia Spears..."

He rattled off a case number.

That was me!

My heart raced as the officer walked toward me. He snatched

my wrists, used a key to disconnect me from the others, then grumbled, "Move it!"

Nothing was done with care on the other side. The guards, officers, civilians were all rude, short, and impatient when they handled inmates. They never tried to hide their disdain for those of us who were accused of breaking the law.

I shuffled up to the door and walked through and into the bright lights of the courtroom. There was no need for me to look around. I knew no one would be there on my behalf, or so I thought.

As I strolled to the front of the judge, I caught a glimpse of Yesterday and my mother. It was hard to describe how seeing them there made me feel. But the anger seemed to melt away just a little. On the other side of the courtroom, Cooper and Evelyn's attorney stood ready to take me down.

When I went before the judge, he had absolutely no sympathy, mercy, nor patience. Once I was properly identified, my case number verified, and my public defender in place, the judge asked a few questions and waited for me to answer.

My shaky voice responded, saying I understood the charges against me, confirmed that I was aware there was a protective order to stay away from Cooper and my sister, and then I was urged to enter a plea.

"You are hereby sentenced to thirty days in jail," the judge said.

The bang of his gavel brought it all home for me. Was I really about to be in jail for an entire month? What would happen to my jobs, and what about my apartment?

Thinking about my situation disgusted me, because I had come to the realization that I didn't need to go over there. There was no reason I should've showed up at their house, but a part of me just wanted to do it out of spite.

My sister, Evelyn, hated when I came around. I think deep

down, she was afraid I might try and steal Cooper back. If only she knew. There was no way in hell I wanted him back.

I didn't get to speak to Yesterday or my mom, but I did glance their direction as I was led back out the door I had entered.

"With your time already served, we can get that down to two weeks," the public defender whispered. I didn't acknowledge the comment, so I just kept walking.

One thing I decided, there was no way in hell I was about to keep doing what I'd been doing. Oh, I'd start telling some stories for sure. Why would I continue to protect Cooper and Evelyn when it was real clear neither of them cared anything about me?; And it wasn't that I wanted to protest them; I really didn't want to put my own business out there.

By the time we made it back to the jail, I was exhausted. I didn't want to be bothered and I was still pissed about having to do time. Granted, I didn't think I'd be there for an entire thirty days, but the fact that I had to be there for something so stupid made me feel, stupid.

Two days after court, Yesterday and I sat in the visiting area.

"So, let me give you an idea of what I'm talking about."

Up to that moment, her words were just that, words. But in a recent phone call, I had asked her to look into some possible interviewing and how much money I could get.

"*Inside Edition* pays on average fifteen to twenty thousand. They'd pay more if he was like a movie star, but trust me when I tell you, there's definitely interest there. And that's not even counting *TMZ* and the other places."

"Are you saying like fifteen thousand dollars?" I was dumbfounded. Now I understood why people sold stories about celebs.

Yesterday nodded.

"You wouldn't listen. I told you, they'll pay for dirt on him. But there is a little bit of a downside."

"What? Having everybody all up in my business?" Sarcasm dripped from each word.

"No, not that, but there is a chance the publicity could make him even more popular."

I smirked. "All the dirt I've got on that heartless dog? I doubt it."

Yesterday shook her head as if she were dealing with naivete.

"Girl, why do you think some of those celebs plant stories about themselves? If nobody is talking about them, they start to feel like they're losing it or something."

Yesterday's expression changed fast. I braced myself.

"Then there's something else too," she said. Suddenly, her focus left me and traveled around the room.

I kept my eyes trained on her. If I was going to do what she'd suggested, I needed to know about all of the possibilities.

"Just listen before you decide not to do it, okay," she started.

I pulled in a deep breath, and gnawed on my bottom lip. I wanted her to just spill it. That fifteen thousand dollars had already started dancing around in my head.

"What is it?"

"Dang, calm down," Yesterday said. "I'm getting to it. I don't want you to overreact."

I huffed.

"It would be best if you did the interview before you get out."

The way she said it told me she knew that would be the deal breaker.

At first, I didn't respond. I stared at her and thought about how I should've known it wouldn't be easy for me to get no damn fifteen-thousand dollars.

"Not only is it easy money, but it's money that you could really use." She was right, I needed that money, and under other circumstances, I'd do whatever to get it, but a jailhouse interview was asking too much.

"Why in here?" My face twisted up as I looked around. "Can they even do interviews in here?"

"Felicia, these companies got money; they can do damn near anything they want."

"But look at me." I threw up my arms. My hair was a mess, and orange was not my color.

"That's what would make it even better. Here you are sitting up in jail because you was trying to see your kid while your ex and your *sister* living large."

"Sounds scandalous." I eased back on the hard plastic chair.

"That's what I'm trying to tell you! Nobody knows how he got to where he is. They all think it was a regular case of client falls for manager, but we know that's the bullshit Evelyn has been peddling for years. You can blow them both up, and make a few dollars, but the revenge you get will be priceless."

Chapter Twenty-Six

Y ou probably wouldn't be able to tell by watching TV, but sitting under the tall lights was so hot, it felt like buckets of sweat was pouring down the sides of my face.

My desperate need for money was the only reason I had agreed to do the interview in jail. As I sat underneath the lights that felt more like heat lamps, I instantly regretted my decision.

The agreement was that I would be paid $15,000. It could have been more like $1 million; that's how badly I needed the money.

As people buzzed around the interviewer and me, I had to remind myself that I really needed the money. But the entire thing was way more of a production than I expected.

My nerves started to go bad in the pre-interview. But they were shot to shit by the time the first heating lamp was flicked on.

I didn't know what questions she was going to ask, didn't know what I would say, but Yesterday's words kept ringing out in my head.

Tell them about some of the lowdown shit he's done.

Remember how many times you walked in on him with some THOT.

This is not the time to worry about putting your business out there; let it all hang out.

How do you trash somebody you did dirt with, without trashing yourself? That was back-to-back trash, and I was bound to come out looking dirty too.

My focus returned to the lady who sat across from me when she finally looked at me and asked, "You okay?"

Her trendy blond locks seemed to glisten beneath the light

lamps. The vibrant red top seemed to pop against her golden-tanned skin, and her makeup was flawless. She looked so polished, I felt awkward.

I shifted in my chair and tried to look as presentable as possible. The truth was, everyone would know I was in jail, I had no make-up on, my hair looked bad, and I felt worse. But Yesterday insisted that this would get me the most sympathy. It wasn't that I needed sympathy, but I needed to get people's attention.

Nothing I had tried had worked, so maybe I needed to talk more about my life with Coop. Every time I looked up, he and my damn sister were on TV looking like the chocolate version of a perfect couple.

All of a sudden, the lady looked up into the camera and started to speak.

My heart thumped. What happened to the warning or even a countdown? My eyes grew wide as I sat silent and listened to her introduction.

"The former wife of Houston singing sensation Cooper Spears was arrested Thursday after a judge found her in contempt of court. She remains here in the Harris County jail. The civil matter is the latest in their legal fight that has gone on for several years. Their marriage in the spotlight of Spears' career spanned sixteen years, then ended in a bitter custody battle and divorce in 2010."

I swallowed hard as I listened to her talk about me as if I wasn't sitting right across from her. I folded and unfolded my hands; my palms were damp. Suddenly, my throat felt scratchy like I might lose my voice. But that didn't seem to matter; she talked enough for us.

"That divorce case is sealed and under a gag order," she said, paused, looked down at her notes, then back up at the camera again. "Felicia Spears is now serving thirty days behind bars, and says she wanted to tell her side of the story, and that's why we're here with her inside the Harris County jail."

Did she really need to keep saying I was in jail, we were at the jail? My orange jumpsuit made it obvious where we were.

"Uh, I didn't violate any court orders," I said. "This is about 'You're not supposed to be talking to anybody about your divorce.' That's what they're saying. And, I'm like, this is America, isn't it?"

The woman looked at me slightly baffled. Then she started to speak again.

"Spears says she showed up at court without an attorney because she can't afford one, adding that Cooper was in court with a legal team and an entourage."

"Well, I mean, I wasn't expecting a four-hour hearing without an attorney," I said. "Am I angry? Yes, I missed years of my son's life, and I can't get those years back."

"So what do you want to happen here?" she finally looked at me and asked.

"I want my fair share. I worked hard to help Cooper get his success. I was there when he was a nobody, I made sacrifices, and now this is how I'm treated? It's not right."

"What kind of sacrifices are we talking about?"

I looked into the camera, and took a deep breath.

"Well, he's not the man you all think he is. He sings all these songs about finding the perfect mate and being the man of every woman's dreams, but he's so far from that, it's crazy to think about."

She leaned in.

"What are you saying about the popular R&B singer Cooper Spears?" Her eyebrows raised as her lips formed a tight, thin line. She waited.

My heart raced uncontrollably, and I wasn't sure why I was so nervous. Everything I said was the truth. This was my reality.

"The number of times I walked in on Cooper with other women is ridiculous!"

Her brows danced upward some more. I could tell I was no longer invisible to her. It was obvious I had piqued her interest.

"It was like he couldn't help himself."

"Hell, he's married to my own damn sister right now."

"He's married to your sister?"

The expression on her face was one of great confusion. But I knew she was putting extras on it for the cameras.

"Yes, same mother and father. He and Evelyn acted like they were working on his career, when in fact, they were working on their future, while we were still married."

Her well made-up eyes widened dramatically.

"Your own sister?" she repeated with so much emphasis, it sounded as sinister and scandalous as she intended.

"Yes, my own sister; Cooper has no moral compass, none whatsoever. They were screwing each other right under my nose."

She looked bewildered, so I continued.

"I remember one time, I was working to try and set up a gig for him, and was having a hard time. I couldn't figure out why the promoter kept ignoring my calls. When I finally met with him face to face, he told me that his wife, who actually ran the business, didn't want to do business with such a whoremonger."

"He's a whoremonger? That's a very powerful claim," she said.

Every revelation caused her face to morph into an emotional expression that was more dramatic than the last.

"If women weren't showing up at my house, they were hanging around the clubs where he performed. And I don't blame them as much as I blame him. Coop knew he was married, and I get it:

temptation is real, but he took those vows, not the women looking for a good time."

"If it was so bad, why did you stay in the marriage?"

Her question made me pause. I couldn't tell her that I was screwing around too. The difference between my infidelity and his, was I was doing it to advance *his* career. But it seemed the harder I worked to make him a star, the more he screwed around.

"I had invested too much time, and hard work. Besides, we were a family, and I thought we could work through it all. I tried to go to counseling, but Coop was only concerned about his career. He didn't want to focus on anything but his career."

"What would you say to his fans who may not believe you?"

"Cooper Spears is a serial cheater, child abuser and bigamist who conned me out of my fair share of his newly found fortune."

"Those are very serious charges," she said. Again, her expression was one of great exaggeration. I guess that made for great TV. As she spoke, she split her focus between eye contact with me, her notes, and the camera lens.

"Yes, and every single word is true. I don't need to lie. Coop's adultery nearly drove me to a mental breakdown."

Chapter Twenty-Seven

Back in my cell, I stretched out on the bed and thought back to the interview. Talking about Cooper and all he had done brought back so many memories. And those memories only made me hate myself for being so gullible.

Maybe gullible was too harsh. I was more guilty of trying anything to help Cooper keep his gig. When he had stormed out of the office and asked why I was talking to Lenny, I wanted to bitch-slap him. He needed to understand I was trying to keep him working, but as always, Cooper never thought about what it took to get him where he was; he just wanted to get there. Everything in me wanted to go in on him right there in the hallway.

Instead, I tried to usher Lenny down the hall quickly. I hoped he'd overlook the anger that it was obvious Cooper clung to.

"Felicia, we like doing business with you, but if you can't get him under control, y'all gon' need to find a new home."

"You better hope I wanna come back up in this bitch!" Cooper had the nerve to say over his shoulder.

Lenny looked at me, and the expression on his face was a combination of anger and disgust.

"Bounce then!" he yelled in Cooper's direction. Cooper dismissed his comment with the wave of an arm as he strutted past.

"Quit testing your weight, and be a man. You wanna keep threatening to leave; don't just bounce," Lenny said.

Thank God, Cooper had nearly rounded the corner by the time Lenny finished.

Alone with Lenny, I really didn't want to talk about Cooper anymore, but I knew it couldn't be avoided.

"We're gonna pick up the pace in the second set." I wanted to take the focus away from that messy exchange between the two men, but Lenny wasn't having it.

"This is that bullshit I'm talking about when it comes to Coop and how he carries it around here. That punk ain't doing none of us a favor," Lenny said.

It was clear that Lenny struggled to contain the anger he felt. I knew if he had it his way, Cooper would've been gone. I rubbed Lenny's shoulder and tried my best to channel calm his way.

"You, you good peoples, Felicia, no doubt, but that client of yours, he can eat shit and croak for all we care around here. And that ain't just me talkin', either. Nobody likes his ass. He really needs a good reality check. Like he needs to understand he ain't the only mofo who can hold a tune."

"I'm gonna talk to him, Lenny. I promise you that. Let us get through tonight, and I'm gonna talk some sense into him. We like it here, and I don't need him fucking things up."

Lenny gave me a knowing look, then suddenly, as if he could no longer fight it, a reluctant grin spread across his face. "And he is a fuck-up for sure!"

"Can the church say, 'Amen'!"

We hollered together. The relief that washed over me was more than any words could express. Inside, I gave myself a massive pat on the back because all it would take was one single phone call from Lenny to Al, and our shit would implode. Cooper would be tossed faster than his temper.

Twenty minutes into Cooper's second set, I finally felt some true ease. Club customers were dancing, singing along, and the bar was busy. Lenny didn't have to say anything for me to know he was happy.

That was the thing about Cooper. He was talented; nobody could take that away from him. But his attitude was worse than dry dog shit. It was almost like he intentionally went out of his way to be the asshole he thought he needed to be.

Midway through song number five, a really upbeat dance number, I noticed a woman near the front of the stage. She had a tiny waist, and massive hips and was top heavy.

Normally, the groupies didn't faze me much; I understood they came with the territory. But this chick, was doing way too much.

Her eye contact with Cooper was so intense, it made me a little uncomfortable. I moved around the room and kept an eye on the other partygoers who seemed to be enjoying themselves.

"Felicia, you got a sec?" I nearly went into cardiac arrest at the sound of Lenny's question. My attention was on the night's groupie and the rest of the crowd, so he caught me off guard.

When I looked up, Lenny beckoned me with the wave of a hand.

"Bitnez," he said as he motioned with his head.

I took one last look around before I followed him down the hallway. It couldn't have been another problem with Cooper. He'd been on the stage for nearly thirty minutes.

"Earlier I wanted to tell you this, but Cooper's ignorant ass pissed me off so bad, it slipped my mind."

Lenny opened the small office door and waited for me to walk in.

Cooper hit a high note that I knew was sure to be a crowd-pleaser. His voice was magic. The crowd roared, and I felt good knowing that he still took his craft seriously.

"What's up, Lenny?"

"We've got this review coming up soon, and I thought Cooper could headline." He shook his head. "Now, we don't need none of that pre-Madonna behavior, but every couple of years, we do a review and invite some important record-label types to sit in on the gigs."

My eyes lit up. This could be the break I needed to get Cooper to the next level.

"Now, it showcases our talent, but also how we do things around here, so it's really a win-win if you look at it the right way."

"Yeah, Lenny, I'm listening."

"But here's the thing: the headliner needs to be right. We talking three sets, Friday, Saturday and Sunday nights, starting at six. It's a good opportunity to be seen. We've had some pretty big names come through here and got some real good connections from our showcases."

Lenny didn't have to sell me on the showcase. I understood the importance of it, and I had already heard about its reputation and what it had done for some other Houston alums—Destiny's Child, Hi-Five and several others. As he spoke, all I thought about was making sure Cooper didn't mess things up.

The conversation with Lenny took all of fifteen minutes. I was so excited about the opportunity, I couldn't wait to let Cooper know.

My timing was perfect as I heard the saxophone player doing a solo, so that meant Cooper was either in the bathroom or had left the stage for a quick drink. I left Lenny in the office to do some paperwork and rushed down the hall and toward the club area when I caught a glimpse of light from the dressing room door.

"I'd better turn that off before Lenny start asking us to share a cut on the electric bill." I chuckled to myself as I grabbed the knob and opened the door.

"Oh shit, Licia!"

I heard him before I even saw him. In one quick move, Cooper shoved the groupie's head to the side and swung his leg over.

"What the fuck!" I bellowed, thoroughly disgusted.

"Wait, Felicia, I can explain, I can explain," he yelled.

The chick lay back on her butt and used the back of her hand to wipe her mouth. She didn't seem the least surprised or even uncomfortable.

As Cooper hobbled toward me and tried to zip his fly, I slapped the side of his head and threw one knee to his groin. I could tell I had missed, but he still hunched over and released a hearty groan.

"Damn, Felicia! Why you tripping and shit; I said I could explain!"

Next, I turned my anger to the groupie who sat and stared at everything as if she had no common sense.

"You get your nasty tramp ass outta here before I have the bouncers toss you out."

"What you mad at me for?" She got up from the floor and tried to adjust her top. Her big, beefy breasts flopped as she moved. "You act like he your man or something!" She rolled her eyes as she pieced her little skimpy outfit together.

"Bitch, he's my goddamn husband!"

Finally, some shame and humility clouded her features. She stammered back a bit.

"Uh, I had no idea."

"It's not your job to know; it's his!" I looked over at Cooper who had recovered a little from the half beating I'd put on him. "Get your ass together, and close out this show before you get us fucking fired!"

Chapter Twenty-Eight

For most people, $15,000 probably wasn't a lot of money, but for me, it was about to be a whole new beginning. It wouldn't give me the life I deserved, but it would help make things a bit easier, if only for a few months.

As I sat on the phone with Yesterday, I couldn't help but think about the money I'd get from the first interview I had done.

"See, we've started something," she said.

"What do you mean?"

"They've been publicizing the upcoming interview about Cooper, and it's all everyone is talking about. I think we can try to get in a couple more before it airs."

I liked how Yesterday stayed on her hustle trying to make sure I made the most of what she saw as a real opportunity for me. It wouldn't get me back on a level field with Cooper and Evelyn, but she was right that it would make me feel better. The interview hadn't even aired yet, and I was already feeling pleasure. The weight of my story was just the beginning; it felt good to know that someone other than Yesterday and I knew about the real Cooper.

"Why are they waiting so long to air it?"

"Oh, I asked and the producer told me this was part of their procedure, so it's nothing on you. Legal has to clear it before they air it, but that ain't gonna hold up your money."

"Good, because after I get out of here, I'm gonna need that and then some."

"Well, I went by and talked to your landlord. He says he's gonna hold the place for you. I wish I could say the same about your job."

Yesterday actually looked sad and spoke cautiously.

"I already knew that was coming," I told her. And I did. My job at the call center was not important, so they just usher bodies in and out. They probably had me replaced before the judge's gavel banged.

"Your supervisor from the night job said you could come back as soon as you got back from Mississippi, though."

"Mississippi?" I checked.

"Yeah, girl, that's where your disabled grandmother lived. And when she died, you had to go down there to help straighten things out."

I laughed so hard, tears came to my eyes. Yesterday knew she could lie real good. Even if I had taken my time, I would not have been able to make up some detailed shit like that and make it sound believable. Her attention to detail with the lie was too much.

"Okay, so Mississippi," I said.

"Yeah, and I need you to remember that you had to take care of your grandmother's affairs. Don't go back up in there acting like you didn't know you was helping your kinfolk and make me into a liar."

"Yes, ma'am!" For all the times she pissed me off by riding Cooper's jock, and even still, talking to my mother, these were the times I really appreciated our friendship.

Her visit I didn't want proved that she had been busy on my behalf while I was away in Mississippi.

"So, I'll see if we can get another interview set up for Saturday. And shoot, you'll be out soon, so it's all good."

"Yesterday." I started to choke up. "I really appreciate everything you're doing to help. I guess I'm just trying to say thanks, girl."

I didn't want to be crying during our visit.

"For what?"

Silence hung between us. I gave her a knowing look, tried to compose myself and said, "For everything, you've done a lot to help me."

"Yeah, well, I hope you remember that when you see me jamming to one of Cooper's hit songs. I want you to remember all of this, you hear me?" she joked.

"I hear you."

"But on a serious tip," she said. "Now that I know how you feel, I can and will cut back on his music, because you are right about that. I'm sorry. I never meant to hurt you."

One of the main problems with being in jail was having to be told what to do. They told us when to eat, sleep, shit, and everything else. I was grateful that I wouldn't have to stay for thirty calendar days, but I needed my time to come quickly. Since I wasn't a violent offender, they agreed to shave seven days off the sentence. Of course, I wanted them to shave off two weeks, and give me time served for the rest of the sentence. After the interview on Saturday, I'd have four days before I'd be free.

On my bed, I stared at the ceiling and mentally begged sleep to come. Two women were in a corner playing cards, another was reading a book, and two were braiding hair. I hated being held in a cage like that, but I was glad the area I was in was relatively calm and quiet. And it wasn't a literal cage, but a large room with vomit-colored walls, no windows to the outside, and several rows of bunk beds.

For the most part, we stayed to ourselves. I didn't want to be there long enough to get to know any of the other women on a personal level. I overheard conversations about hooking up on the outside and plans to meet each other's families. All I could think was, who'd want to keep the memory of jail fresh on their mind.

If I ever saw any of these women on the outside, I'd act like I'd never set eyes on them before. My plan was to stay the hell away from jail and everything that reminded me of it—especially the ratchet-ass women who behaved like this was the norm for them.

As I made that promise of no return to myself, thoughts of

Cooper came to mind. It wouldn't be easy to do, but I had to find a way to move past him.

When my eyelids began to feel heavy, I felt incredible joy. But the joy didn't last long as thoughts of my hateful sister crept to mind.

It was day two of the talent review at Milan's of Houston, and I had already claimed a small victory because we made it through Friday without any incidents. Surprisingly, Cooper was on his best behavior, and I beamed with pride.

My thought was, it was Saturday night, so we had made it more than halfway through the showcase. I also played my manager role to the fullest.

"Hi, I'm Felicia Monroe, and I represent Cooper Spears, this year's headliner."

It felt incredible to be able to say I managed the headliner. Of course these people had no clue about the nightmare said headliner could be, and that didn't matter. I was just eager to make a possible connect that could lead to something tangible for his career.

"He's got a good voice and a great look," a man in an expensive suit said. Except for the few seconds he glanced at me, he kept his eyes glued to Cooper. I couldn't remember the man's name, but his positive feedback about Cooper made me linger. I didn't want to appear too desperate, but I also wanted to express interest.

"Yeah, he sounds good, real contemporary; it's what's in right now."

He seemed to enjoy the song as he moved to the beat in his chair.

"Unfortunately, I'm desperate for a sax player right now."

My heart sank at the sound of that.

"But let me give you my card; things change, sometimes without much notice at all."

I accepted his card and prepared to move on to the next table when the sight a few tables over stopped me cold.

Chapter Twenty-Nine

"So I guess you gon' peddle your wares to everybody in here except me, huh?" Her icy words hit me before I could approach her table, but she was right. I had seen her there, and didn't plan to stop. That was the problem with something like this; there was no limit to whom you'd see.

"Bitch, don't play; this is my business. It's high stakes poker, and I ain't got time for none of your games."

"Your business, huh." She threw her head back and laughed, then looked around in her signature bitchy manner. "Well, it's clear you don't know what the hell you're doing, as usual." She rolled her eyes.

In order to keep it professional and not blow whatever opportunity may have been available to Cooper, I tried to keep moving, but it was obvious, I had little control over others' lack of professionalism.

Unfortunately for me, Lenny walked up before I could fire back at that low blow Evelyn had made about my lack of skills. She was lucky too because it was about to go down.

"Oh, Felicia, this is Evelyn Malone; she's a scout for Sony. I really wanted you two to meet."

I was a little nervous that he might make the connection, but he didn't, so I played along. My mind floated to a thought. Since when did Sony have scouts? The smile on my face was for Lenny alone, and I knew for sure that Evelyn was aware. She may have been full of shit, but was also stupid and that made for a bad combination.

The hatred between Evelyn and me went back to early childhood.

As the youngest, she commanded all of the attention and all of the little privileges that should've been divided equally between us. Even back then, she was all about self and cared nothing about what others thought.

It wasn't just that she was convinced she was the pretty one, but more that she always behaved as if everyone owed her something. And when she couldn't get it from most people, she'd damn near kill herself to try and take it from me. That was the nature of our relationship: she took, and took, and took, until it was all gone.

Although we were only four years apart, by the time Evelyn came along, my mother was tired and that meant I took over lots of responsibilities that should have had nothing to do with me. It was like Evelyn was my child, despite that I had done nothing to have her. I hated her because all she did was take from me. When she walked into a room, what little if any attention I had, was gone instantly. She'd try to take the air I breathed if she thought there was any value in her having it.

As I eyed her suspiciously, I hoped that would be enough for her to retreat, and keep quiet. But I knew better.

Evelyn ignored my deathly stare, boldly stood anyway, used her hands to smooth down her dress, then said, "You manage the headliner, right? He's pretty good. His voice, he's got the right look, a real complete package."

I wanted to knock her back down in that chair, but in Lenny's presence, I had no choice but to grin and nod.

"Yeah, you'll find some of the country's best hidden talent here at Milan's of Houston," Lenny said proudly.

He, like most men in our presence, was all too eager to try and please Evelyn. She dressed to thrill; her clothes were always the best of the best. As a teen, she would save every dime she got her hands on, including allowances, and birthday money, so she could go buy the best knockoffs on Harwin.

"I enjoyed his set last night, and it was even better tonight. You got something real in that one there," Evelyn said. Her thirst was very apparent.

"Yeah, ole Coop is really good. The bastard can sang his ass off, for sure," Lenny said. He laughed and I understood the turbulent relationship that existed, but I was glad to know that when the time came, Lenny knew how to put aside their differences and say positive things about a fucked-up individual like Cooper.

I stood silent as they talked about Cooper. I wasn't sure what she was up to and why she'd come back home, but I wasn't about to fall for her shit. If I knew anything about my sister, for sure, her agenda would mean trouble for me.

"You know, I haven't been home in years. If I knew this was the kind of raw talent you all had up in here, I would have been put this spot in my rotation," Evelyn said.

"That's what we want you to do, make us part of your routine. Don't sleep on Milan's of Houston." Lenny laughed. I wondered whether he was the same man who wanted to put his foot up in Cooper's ass. "And wait, H-town is home for you?"

"Yup, Northside bred and reared. 'Gunspoint,' Humble, I know all the hot spots," Evelyn boasted.

"Hotdamn! I didn't know you was a home-girl! That's what's up!" Lenny slapped his thigh with the excitement of the news that Evelyn was a Houston native. I wanted to roll my eyes hard enough for them all to see, but I refrained.

"Yeah, but you know, I move differently these days," she boasted.

"Okay, I see, I see. Ain't nothing wrong with that, baby girl. That just means you a few steps ahead of these other jokers, right."

"Believe that. I used to be all about these streets. See, these white boys, they don't usually know where to find the good stuff, but this right here," she waved her arms around, "All of this screams me."

With all the bullshit flying around, I didn't even notice Cooper when he snuck up on us. That was the thing about being around Evelyn; she threw me off my game and made me second-guess myself. Despite all the years that had gone by, nothing had changed when it came to that. And I didn't know whether I hated her or myself more for it.

Lenny's cell phone rang. "Excuse, I gotta take this," he said before he left. I was glad I didn't have to endure him and Cooper in such close proximity.

But, while I was glad a call took Lenny away, I didn't want to be left alone with Evelyn. And despite Cooper's presence, I may as well have been alone. Cooper was always about team self, especially if he caught a hint of a possible opportunity.

"Who's this, Licia?" my husband asked. His voice startled me, since I was already off my game.

He had never met my sister because the bitch was too important and too busy to come home for our wedding. And once she'd built her new life, her country folk didn't fit into her new persona. Evelyn had left for New York right after high school and never looked back. Her calls were frequent in the beginning when she needed money, but it didn't take long for those to become less frequent, until they all but stopped.

The tone of Cooper's voice didn't say business when he inquired about her, and that made me even more uncomfortable.

Before I could answer, Evelyn stepped forward, slightly in front of me, and offered Cooper a dainty jeweled hand. "I'm the woman who's about to change your life." She grinned so hard, I could see the bridge in the back of her mouth.

Cooper's right eyebrow inched upward. The thirst in his eyes was so embarrassing, he made my stomach churn. He was like a kid who needed to be reminded of stranger danger constantly, but he still wouldn't listen, especially if he thought he could benefit.

"Listen, Evelyn, if you want to talk business, we can set up an appointment for next week and discuss the logistics." I tried to intervene.

Cooper was so stupid, he couldn't even tell when I was trying to throw him a lifeline. There was no synergy between us, and that made working together even more of a challenge. I tried to send all kinds of nonverbal warnings, but as usual, he was too busy trying to decide whether he needed to prostitute himself to make something happen.

"Who you with?" Cooper asked before I could finish the word logistics. His brows knitted together in deep concentration.

When she said Sony, I knew for a fact he probably creamed himself a little.

Chapter Thirty

O ne month after the showcase, my life was hardly recognizable. By now, we had moved into a small, one-bedroom apartment, but still spent the majority of our time at my mom's because she watched Trey. My marriage and our business relationship were strained.

It was like Cooper had lost all confidence in my ability to handle his career. As the days went on, his behavior continued to baffle and piss me off at the same time.

I was accustomed to working alone, but I had convinced myself that even through his constant complaints, we were somewhat of a team. However, now, we no longer discussed strategy; we didn't review the gigs or even brainstorm about ways to get his name out there. He behaved as if we were no longer a team. He never asked about the city events, the more high-brow gigs he was once hungry to get, or anything else at all.

Now, when I presented a gig, he wasn't interested. He'd simply say, "No, not gonna happen." There was no explanation, no complaints, and no more conversation. A few times, I had looked like a fool having to circle back to cancel something I had set up. The difference in Cooper was nothing less than stunning. But the ultimate betrayal blindsided me.

One afternoon, he burst into my mom's house at an hour that he should've been driving a Metro bus, and I was really exasperated. Nothing good could come from him being off in the middle of the afternoon. Cooper was unreachable on an ordinary business day, so for him to come home early meant something had gone wrong.

With wide and wild eyes, I waited for an explanation even though I already suspected trouble. Although I couldn't think of any explanation that would be worthy, I still waited. There was nothing patient about my demeanor as I listened to the gibberish that flowed from his mouth.

"Eve said I should quit my job, and that's exactly what I did. She said I need to dedicate all of my time toward my singing."

He made the announcement with such conviction that I almost thought he was performing for a hidden camera or something, or setting me up for the punchline to a bad joke. But he was serious. He was really excited that he had quit a job he'd worked so hard to maintain. It took close to forever for him to get the coveted day shift, and here he had gone and quit? And he'd quit, without even talking to me.

There were no words to express the anger I felt. And what made the moment even worse, my mom was no help at all.

"So, you just quit? I mean, just like that, did you give them notice or anything?" she asked.

Cooper shook his head, saying no. "What Eve said makes so much sense. If I devoted as much time to my singing as I did driving those buses, helping to build somebody else's dream, who knows where I'd be right now." He cut his eyes at me.

So now, being a city bus driver was helping someone else's dream? How could he not see that his job was our family's income? I didn't work because for us, child care was too out of reach early on, and even as Trey got older, Cooper needed me to be available to help him.

"But to not give any notice," my mother said, her voice sounding uncertain.

There was a small glimmer of hope in her statement, and I thought for a second, she'd be able to talk some sense into him, or at least allow him to see how reckless his behavior had been.

Cooper moved closer to my mother. "Knowing I cannot go back to that job is going to be the fuel to keep me grinding. I quit on the spot and told them I was about to follow my dream."

It had to be one of the stupidest moves ever. I stood silent in stunned disbelief as he went on about having confidence and faith in his dream.

I just couldn't fathom how being unemployed would advance his career. But my simple, star-hungry whore of a husband was too dumb to think for himself.

"Besides, people step out on faith every single day. And when I told my immediate supervisor, he actually said he understood, and he was proud of me."

That was all Tabitha needed to hear. Without missing a beat, Tabitha immediately switched positions and was once again his cheerleader.

"Just give it to God—wait, pray, and repeat," my mother had the nerve to say.

"Just pray?" I threw up my hands. I didn't care how upset he was. I could no longer sit by and listen to the foolishness.

Their heads flew in my direction as if they finally realized I was still in the room.

"Are you doubting God's ability?" my mother asked as she craned her neck to look around my husband at me. She looked thunderstruck that I'd consider going against God.

After a healthy huff, I said, "No, I'm not questioning God; I'm questioning Coop's actions based on Eve's dumb-ass advice. Think about it, would God want someone to quit a decent paying job that was supporting his family before he secured another one? God don't say anything about having and using good common sense?"

"Licia, ever since I've been listening to Eve, it's like you trying to find things to complain about. If I didn't know any better, I'd have to question whether you really want me to make it."

My eyes grew wider at his accusation.

"Eve's advice is always so sporadic, nothing is well thought out, she's flying from the seat of her damn pants, and there's no safety net. But the worst part is, she's got you following each and every single word, and you don't see the disaster that's headed your way."

"The woman told me to quit, so I can focus more on my singing career. We're not gonna get anywhere with me working a mind-numbing nine-to-five job."

He actually shook his head at me, as if it was I who was clueless. But he quit his damn job, with no real plan.

"Coop, why can't you see the mistake you're making here? So, you quit your job; outside of the gig at Milan's, what other income do *we* have? What about supporting our family? And what the hell are you going to do all day now that you're unemployed?" I was beyond pissed; it took everything I could muster up to speak calmly. "I'm all for stepping out on faith, but God also don't want you to make stupid decisions."

Regardless of how much sense my comments made, all Coop heard and understood was what he wanted.

"Eve said I need to be taking voice lessons during the day. She also said you need to work to secure some additional gigs and help me get more exposure."

"'Eve said,' 'Eve said.' I'm so sick and tired of Eve and every damn thing she said. Where is she gonna be when our bills are due?"

Just like a bad dream in which the villain appears at the mention of their name, there was a soft knock before the door flew open.

"Hey, Mama," Eve sang as she sauntered into the room.

She glanced at my son, smiled and greeted my husband, but left the best for me. Her evil stare would have killed me, had me buried six feet under, before my family was even notified of my sudden and unexpected death.

"Wait, don't tell me; you probably over here second-guessing every single piece of advice I've given Coop." The twisted expression on her face remained long after the insult.

"You tell my husband to quit his job, knowing he doesn't have another one, talking some bullshit about stepping out on faith, and you're wondering whether I'm second-guessing you?"

Eve threw her hands to her hips and stood firm as if she were prepared for battle.

"Then, in addition to being unemployed, he's supposed to take voice lessons daily? How the hell are we gonna pay for that, and why does he need voice lessons?" I rolled my eyes so hard, if they'd fallen from their sockets, they would've flown across the room.

While I expected some type of bullshit response from Eve, nothing could've prepared me for the next words she delivered. It felt like they were designed to knock me out cold, and that's exactly what they did.

"It's okay. I anticipated this, and that's why I had a real good talk with Coop. And after our talk, Coop has asked me to take over the management of his career," she said with a straight face. "I told Coop, he made the right choice, and we are going to be a great team."

Chapter Thirty-One

As I held the phone and sat on hold, I wondered why it was near impossible to verify Evelyn's so-called credentials. I tried to find out whether her job with Sony was legit, but it was more difficult than I expected.

After being bounced around to various departments, either placed on hold or transferred to the wrong person, my patience was running thin. My gut told me that I was on to something when I decided to check her out, so I tried to be patient.

And if she were legit, why was it so difficult to verify that she worked for the company? It wasn't like I didn't have the necessary information needed for the verification. I knew her full government name, her date of birth, and any other pertinent information they might need.

"Ma'am, who did you say you're with again?" the fifth person I'd spoken to from Sony Music came back on the line and asked.

"Uh, my group is trying to make sure someone we met really is who she says she is," I stammered.

Completely unprepared to be questioned about my own intentions threw me off a bit, but I bounced back instantly.

"Okay, well, we do employment verifications frequently. Give me a name, and I'll tell you whether they're employed by Sony Music."

I quickly gave up Evelyn's name, date of birth, and was about to offer up her social security number when the woman stopped me. "Yes, Evelyn Malone is employed by Sony Music; she works in

A&R. So, if you met her at any type of gig or an open mic event, you can rest assured, she's just doing her job."

"Oh, okay, well, thank you."

The lump that was suddenly lodged in my throat felt like a boulder. So, she was legit, damn. I was disappointed in both the time I'd wasted and the confirmation that her job was legit.

"No problem, can I help you with anything else?" the woman asked cheerfully.

Can you kill the bitch, chop her body into small pieces, and spread them out in deep, shark-infested waters?

"Uh, no, I think that's it. That's all I needed," I lied.

The woman was pleasant and friendly, despite her devastating information. I wanted desperately for Evelyn to be lying about who she was and what she was doing. It was pitiful that I knew nothing about my sister or her life, but there was nothing I could do to turn her into the lying fraud I needed her to be.

She was now working closely with Coop, so I also had to be careful about trashing her.

"Why didn't you ever tell me much about Eve?" he asked one night.

So, now we're on nickname basis? I threw up a little in my mouth each time he referenced her in a positive manner. And lately, it had been often.

"I told you what I knew about her. She left home and never looked back. Back in the day, I guess she saw Houston as some country city that she needed to get far away from, and we hadn't heard from her in years."

Coop listened intently.

"That's just strange to me how you could be so distant from your own family." He gave me a curious expression. "And to imagine she's really big time."

He had no way of knowing, but that last comment shattered my heart. He sounded so enamored with her, with her status and knowing him, his mind was already working overtime thinking about all that she could do for him.

I didn't want to remind Cooper that he wasn't close to any of his siblings, either, so I let him go on about how weird my family was, how Evelyn was so successful and how he finally felt like things were about to happen.

The excitement in his voice when he talked about her was too much for me to handle, but I told myself he'd find out soon enough that Evelyn was never whom she appeared to be. I didn't give a damn which company had been dumb enough to hire her.

"She had me do some professional headshots, said they're for a new press kit. I really like her; she really knows her shit."

He couldn't see me rolling my eyes. What Cooper failed to see was every time he complimented Eve's skills as it related to his career, it was like insulting me. Essentially, he was saying she was able to accomplish things I could not do.

How was I supposed to know she had established this new life as a record label scout? She literally had cut off her entire family, gone someplace else and recreated herself as if we didn't exist.

"Think about this: in the last two weeks alone, she's basically doubled the number of gigs I've had, and since I left Milan's, it's like everyone wants me."

Cooper knew bringing up Milan's was an especially sore subject for me. I didn't agree with the way Eve had him leave that establishment. He had basically left them hanging and didn't even wait for his replacement.

Evelyn had sweet-talked Lenny and told him and Big Al how she'd be sure they got full credit because she had discovered Cooper there, and they ate it all up.

Everyone was happy and excited. She'd even sold them a bunch of bull about how she'd try to team up with them for a music festival once she got Coop's career off.

As usual, Evelyn had everyone eating all of her shit without asking any questions. It made me sick to my stomach.

"Felicia Spears!"

The guard's loud voice pulled me back to the present and my current situation. For once in many years, I didn't feel despondent.

"C'mon! It's time to go!"

Excitement flooded my veins as I scrambled to gather the little stuff I had accumulated while in jail. I was so ready to be at home in my own damn space. I left what I didn't want and didn't even look back as two women prepared to fight over my discarded belongings.

I knew Yesterday would be waiting for me, and that was a great thing. From the time they called my name to the time I walked out a free woman, it felt like an entire twenty-four hours had lapsed.

While I was so glad to be free, I felt like they could try to make that process faster.

Once outside, it didn't matter that there was no breeze nor wind, and the humidity clung to my skin like a thick coating. I was happy to be out. The air was still as I walked out and took in a huge deep breath. I inhaled and held the smell in my lungs and tried to savor it for as long as possible. Freedom smelled better than it felt, and I was so happy to be free. I moved quickly toward the car, just in case someone realized there was an error and tried to pull me back in.

Quickly, I approached the vehicle, pulled the passenger door of Yesterday's car, climbed in and sank into her seat. I sighed hard.

"Wheew! Thank you so much."

"Girl, please, no need to thank me."

"No, I'm serious. Thank you for everything. Thank you for the advice about the interviews, setting them up, organizing my money, just everything."

"I get it, you all up in your feelings 'cause you been on lock for a minute, but on a serious note, you ain't gotta thank me because I didn't do nothing you wouldn't have done for me."

She was right about that for sure. After a long emotional stretch of silence, we both struggled to fight tears.

Yesterday cranked the car, and pulled into the street. I was quiet for the rest of the ride home, and grateful that Yesterday was playing music from her iPhone and not a single one of Coop's songs was on her playlist rotation.

Chapter Thirty-Two

Yesterday could only drop me off at home because she had something else to do, and couldn't stay to socialize. I didn't mind, I was glad to be out and wanted to be alone to readjust to being home.

"I'll roll through later this evening. Besides, you probably need some alone time to pull yourself back together," she said, reading my mind as I slid out of her car and clutched the envelope and brown paper bag that held the few items I kept.

"Okay, well, I'll be here, so see you later."

It was as if my landlord were watching us because the minute Yesterday pulled off, and I stepped inside the building's common area, he emerged and greeted me. He wasn't overly emotional, but he did manage to show some expression of concern.

"I heard what happened."

Unsure about how I should respond, I tried to act like I needed to concentrate on opening my front door.

"You look good. And I don't wanna be all up in your business, but I'm glad you home."

At the sound of that, I looked him in the eyes. "Thanks, I appreciate it."

"Let me know if you need a little time with next month's rent."

"Thank you, but I should be fine."

"You sure, Felicia? Ain't no need in trying to be all proud. This ain't charity; I just want you to know I understand. Besides, there's something in it for me too. You a good tenant, and I don't wanna lose you."

His concern warmed me, but the fact that I really was good and wouldn't need an extension to pay the rent was even better.

After I finished with him, I opened my door and walked into my small, empty apartment. It wasn't much, but it was mine, it was clean, and I didn't have to worry about fighting other women for space in a cage.

I peeled off the clothes I'd been wearing when I was arrested and wished I owned a fireplace. I wanted to burn them. The scent of jail seemed embedded into the fibers, and I didn't need anything that would remind me of where I had been. Especially since I had no plans to ever go back.

Instead of a shower, I decided I'd do it up like the ladies in the movies and fixed myself a big, bodacious bubble bath. I wasn't hungry, or thirsty; I just had an incredible urge to clean myself.

If I could have put bleach in my bathwater, I would've used an entire gallon. I wanted to get rid of the jail scent that seemed to still seep from my pores.

Since my place was small and clean, I didn't have to do much prep work before the bath. When thoughts of my special cocktail crossed my mind, I thought about how Whitney Houston had died and decided I'd pass on the extras. The bath would have to do.

When I dipped my toe into the water, it felt really hot, but incredibly good, so with caution, I stepped into the tub, lowered my body in, and released a breath when I was able to sit.

I slowly leaned back and laid my head on top of a folded towel. I allowed the music to take me back to the memories I struggled to forget.

Cooper wasn't making a lot of money, but with the gigs Evelyn had arranged, we seemed to make ends meet. We had left my mother's by then, but we were there so much, it was like we hadn't moved into our own apartment. And the apartment was worse than a starter place for students who had done their time in a dormitory, and finally had a place, so it wasn't as if we were making great strides. Without his job, I knew we would be back to living at my mother's, indefinitely. And that thought really pissed me off.

What made the situation worse was, Evelyn felt she had full unchecked access to her client, my husband. She knew no boundaries. To save face and try to get back at them, I had been scouting new talent in hopes of showing her and Cooper that she wasn't the only game in town.

"Oh, Licia, I'm glad you're here, I wanna show you something," Cooper said as I walked into the kitchen. I instantly regretted the decision to enter a room they occupied.

He and Evelyn had all types of pictures, folders, and paperwork spread across the table. The way she carried on, as if she were doing so much work on his behalf, screamed fake and overdoing it. My mother was at the stove where she hovered over a pot.

Cooper insisted on trying to pull me into any discussion or project with Evelyn, and I resisted as much as possible.

He was excited as he adjusted the computer monitor for me to get a better look.

"Eve made sure all my music is up on SoundCloud and YouTube." Envy crept up on me fast.

He used his index fingers to bang on a few keys, then I watched as the screen came to life. There was a performance of Cooper belting out a sultry song about the power of sex. The lyrics and beat were real catchy, and I knew the song would be an instant hit.

What stood out even more than the music and sexually charged lyrics was Cooper himself. I wasn't sure how she'd done it, but there was a spotlight on him that highlighted his skin color and those amazing eyes.

Instantly, I scolded myself because years ago, I had watched

Oprah Winfrey discuss the importance of being seen in the best light possible. She'd talked about how her team specifically adjusted her lighting to make sure she glowed. I wasn't representing a client back then, but that was information I should have remembered. It was something that was simple and made such a tremendous difference. It was something small that would have made a difference with Coop.

Cooper looked amazing in the videos; it was as if he glowed while on stage. He stood out from the band, and it looked like it was all about him.

"That's nice," I said with as much lackluster as possible.

After the second video that looked just as good and polished as the first, he stopped me before I could leave. I was disgusted, but had to act like all was well.

"Wait, I want you to see this. Eve said it's essential that we have synchronization with all of my social media platforms," he said as his index fingers banged on more keys.

"Yes, that's especially important, so we don't confuse your fans by making each one of your social media pages different," she chimed in as if anyone had asked her. While I believe she was speaking to him, she said it in a way that let me know that this was yet another thing that illustrated just how ineffective I had been as my husband's manager.

"That means, my Facebook cover photo is the same as my Twitter header, and my SoundCloud display picture is the same as my website and YouTube display picture. Everything is the same, so now I have a recognizable brand that my fans will be able to see."

He beamed with so much pride as he showed off everything that Evelyn had orchestrated.

"We're really playing catch-up. These are things that should have been done long before now. It's a wonder I found him. These kids are doing this stuff, and they're upping their chances of being discovered. Nowadays, it's not even a must that all of this is done. It's almost like a calling card that speaks about your professionalism and your readiness to play with the big boys."

The things she said sounded great, but the way she said them implied that they should have been common sense, and I, of course, was a loser for having not done them for my client.

And I would have sworn that when our eyes met, and Cooper's were focused on the screen, she taunted me. There was no way I could bother him with the foolishness because of course, he'd take it as me being petty.

Chapter Thirty-Three

Cooper had a photo shoot the next day, and I knew Evelyn would be by trying to taunt me. So I had to work smart. First. I told him that we needed to go to Tabitha's early because she needed his help around the house. That was easy; he'd bend over backward to help my mother. I already had several outfits with his accessories packed.

"What time did you say you needed to be at the studio?" I asked Cooper as I scooped scrambled eggs onto his plate.

"Eleven, I think that's what Evelyn said."

He attacked the biscuits and bacon before I turned my back.

"Oh snap! I'm glad you said something. She called while you were in the bathroom, wanted to know if you could get there an hour earlier, said something about someone she wanted you to meet."

Cooper nearly choked on his food. "Damn, why didn't you tell me that before I sat down to eat?"

I turned around, confusion all over my face. I looked at the clock and waited for him to follow my gaze.

"It's eight forty-five. What's the big deal?"

He jumped up from the table, took a bite of the biscuit sandwich he had created with the eggs and bacon, then washed it all down with juice. He rushed toward the back and yelled over his shoulder, "You just don't get it."

If I didn't want to make sure he was gone when Evelyn arrived like I knew she would, I would tell him just who didn't really get it.

As I washed the dishes, he rushed back in. "How does this look?"

Before I could answer, my mother, who seemed to come out of nowhere, chimed in. "What else you got?"

"I didn't know you were still here," I said to her.

"Yeah, forgot something, but looks like I'm right on time." She looked down at the plate. "Whose food, and is anyone eating it?"

"Ma, you can have it. It was mine, but now I have to hurry and get ready for a photo shoot," Cooper said. I hated when Cooper called my mother Ma, instead of Tabitha.

My mother snatched up the biscuit. "You need to wear red or burgundy. Those colors look good on you—your power colors."

Cooper snapped his fingers.

"See, that's why I like when we were around you more often. But *we* brought a few options," he said, kissing up to her. The grin on her face was spectacular. I rolled my eyes at the two as he left, then returned with a different outfit. He could be worse than the pickiest woman. *We* hadn't brought anything—I had.

By the time he dashed in wearing a wine-colored button-down with detailed designs on the collar, cuffs, and a pair of dark designer jeans, my mother nearly had a fit.

"Now that's what I'm talking about! You look great, son!"

"Thanks, Ma," Coop said.

Again, they behaved as if I wasn't in the room, but I didn't mind. I wanted to save my words for Evelyn anyway.

"I can drop you, if you need me to," my mother offered.

"Oh, that's what's up. I'll be ready to go in five. I can't find my cell."

"Just go, I'll look for it," I said.

Cooper stopped and looked at me. "But what if Evelyn calls?"

"I'll let her know Mom dropped you."

He seemed reluctant at first, but at my mother's urging, he grabbed his bag and rushed to grab the door for her.

"Later, Felicia," my mother said as she walked through the door. "Don't leave no dishes in my sink!"

By the time ten in the morning rolled around, I was good and ready. The doorbell chimed. I rose from the sofa, checked my reflection in the mirror, then pulled the door open.

There was no need to ask who was at the door. I pulled it open and waited for her to walk in. She sauntered in like she were the fucking First Lady of the United States.

"Where's your husband? His cell is going straight to voicemail."

Evelyn strolled straight to the kitchen and never looked around to notice that we were alone. By the time she did, I met her at the doorway with a good firm slap to the side of her face.

She stammered back, grabbed at her cheek and allowed her mouth to hang wide in shock.

"What the hell is your problem?"

"You! If you think I'm about to sit by and let you move in on my husband, you need to think again."

Evelyn rubbed the side of her face, but the shock quickly disappeared, replaced by a smug expression.

"Is that the best you can do?"

I was breathing fire as she straightened her back and seemed to brace herself for my next blow, but I was the one who nearly fell to the floor.

"You don't have to worry about me moving in on Coop; that's already happened. Once he told me about your open marriage, I figured why not. You think I'm gonna invest all of this time and work into some man, so that the two of you can reap the benefits of my hard work?" Evelyn giggled. She dug for a compact and used it to inspect her cheek. "You better be glad that didn't leave a mark. But anyway, as I was saying, Cooper thanks me continuously for the work I do."

My eyes narrowed at her words, and while I wanted desperately to knock Evelyn on her ass, something in me stopped.

"Yeah, so while you over here thinking you need to check me, looks like you should've been checking the man who committed to you."

"You bitch!"

Evelyn's laugh was so loud and wicked she made me even more angry. There was nothing funny about our situation, but still she howled with laughter.

"That's the thing about you desperate wives. Y'all wanna come after the other woman. Honey, ain't no man gonna step out unless he wants to."

Before I could fire back at her comment, she adjusted the strap of her purse on her shoulder, passed by me, with a harder than necessary bump, and walked out.

I wasn't sure what pissed me off more—the bump or what she had said about my so-called open marriage.

By the time I had learned that Evelyn had lied through her teeth, it really was too late. She may not have done the deed with Cooper before that day, but that night, when he failed to come home, I knew that she'd told him about the confrontation, I guess that was his way of letting me know how he felt about what I had done.

Chapter Thirty-Four

"Don't you see what she's trying to do to us?" I asked Cooper the next day when he finally came home. It was more like the next night, and despite that he was the one who should have been begging for mercy, he had a chip on his shoulder the size of a brick.

At first, he walked in and behaved as if he had done nothing wrong. When he finally acknowledged my presence, he did so with a look of disgust. But suddenly, and to my surprise, his features softened, and he changed his expression.

He eased back onto our bed and for a second, I thought maybe I had finally broken through the façade that I was convinced was Evelyn.

"She's messy and that's all it boils down to."

Before I could finish my complaint, the frown had already returned to his face.

"Damn, Licia, why does everything have to be about you? We supposed to be focusing on my career, but yet we keep going back to issues you have with your own damn sister."

"*My* issues with her?"

I was dumbfounded. Had he heard anything I'd said about Evelyn?

"Yeah, man, you waste so much time worrying about what she's doing, how she's doing it, the amount of time we together, that I don't even think you think about my career anymore. And where the fuck you get off slapping her like that?"

"That's how you really feel?"

Without a millisecond of hesitation, he said, "It needed to be said. It needed to be said because you need to stop throwing shade and kill the hate."

Stop throwing shade?

Kill the hate?

"Look, all I'm saying is, either you're Team Spears, or you're flying solo. I don't know how else to put it, so you'll understand."

"So what are you if you going around telling people that we have an open marriage?"

If the question took him by surprise, he didn't flinch.

"Evelyn told me what she said to you, and after you laid hands on her, you better be glad that's all she said." He shook his head.

"Damn, she working her ass off for us, and you go and pull some ole dumb shit like that? Ain't nobody got time for that." He dismissed me with the wave of a hand.

As he basically put me down, I wondered why I hadn't seen it before. Just like she had done with everything I had, Evelyn was trying to take my man.

"This ain't got nothing to do with making you a star, Coop; this is what Evelyn has always done. You are *my* husband, married to me. She ain't got one, so what does she do? She tries to take mine, like she's always done."

Cooper's laugh was so hearty, I wasn't sure whether he was faking it. That was the thing that drove me crazy about being around Evelyn. She had a way of putting everyone in a mood.

My husband looked at me like I had grown a third eyeball.

"So you on some ole 'she stole my boyfriend' bull?"

From his side of the bed, he gave me a look that said he wasn't buying any of my revelation when it came to Evelyn. He sighed hard and loud as if it were all he could do to have to go over this with me again.

"Licia, you said yourself, she left home and never looked back, but suddenly years later, she decides she wants a man, so she passed up all the eligible bachelors between L.A. and Texas and came back home to Houston, after all these years and decided she wanted *your* husband." His words were soaked in sarcasm.

I rolled my eyes and blew out a hard breath. He wouldn't hear me out. He wouldn't listen even though I was trying to tell him what I was witnessing. Evelyn wanted to do more than make him a star, and I doubted that she could actually do that.

But he couldn't be bothered.

Our days and nights started to look different. We passed each other, many times with few words between us. It hurt my heart the way he ignored all of the signs I tried to show him.

"I got a gig tonight," he announced after I had put our son to sleep one night.

It made little sense to me that he would be telling me at the last minute that he had a gig. I had felt something wasn't right.

"Oh, let me call my mom. I'm gonna go with you, so she can keep an eye on the baby."

The reaction he gave me was so unexpected, that it threw me.

"Eve said you might want to come tonight."

I whipped around and had to catch myself. In that moment, I asked God to soften my words because I was about to go in about what *Eve said*. God answered my prayers because instantly, I regrouped and asked, "Where are we going?"

It was hard to tell whether he was as surprised by my reaction as I was by his. If he was, he didn't skip a beat. He finished fiddling with his shirt, then looked over at me and said, "I'll call her and ask. I forgot, it was a last-minute thing." He shrugged.

There was no need for me to go with them, but I couldn't back out. I wasn't curious about Cooper's new gigs, especially since I already knew about the changes she'd made.

It was strange how Cooper went out of his way to keep me updated, but rarely asked for my input or opinion on anything Evelyn suggested. It was as if her words were the gospel, and once spoken, his only mission was to follow through on her suggestions.

His behavior made me wonder whether he got some kind of pleasure out of dangling everything Evelyn was doing in front of me. And that's what he did. If Evelyn told him to piss sitting down, he'd let me know, then rush and do it. The entire situation was maddening.

As things progressed with them, I found myself trying too hard to find a talent as good as Coop. There was Milkdrop. Every time I heard his name, I rolled my eyes. He was an R&B artist trapped in a rapper's persona. The problem was I wasn't interested in having a rapper as a client.

Milkdrop's voice was okay, nothing much to talk about, but at least he could hold a note. But he had other issues.

"Yo, look all around you. Yo, rap is straight taking over; e'erybody is rapping, Yo." He wore his skinny jeans that sagged beneath his butt and showed off his boxers, had sleeves (tattoos from his fingertips to the top of his shoulders), and always wore a cap turned backward with a bandana underneath. The bandana covered his long cornrows.

Then there was Seduction. She was in her mid-twenties, nice-looking, but with her, the elevator refused to go all the way to the top.

"I think we need to promote me like they did Britney," she'd say.

When I'd suggested she needed more voice work, her response was simple.

"Miss Felicia, you need to get with the times; ain't nobody trying to be like Aretha Franklin, Anita Baker, or any of those old ladies you used to. If you get me some studio time, they can make me sound good enough to get us a deal, and make me a star."

That was the mentality I was dealing with. I visited talent shows, open mic events, spoken word events, and anything else I could find that showcased talent. The problem was, talent was subjective, and a lot of the younger people I encountered felt they deserved fame without any real talent or even any effort.

"So, you hear Evelyn say we probably need to take a trip to L.A.? She got some real important people she wants me to meet."

That's when the moon could've dropped from the sky.

Chapter Thirty-Five

B y the time my interview hit the airwaves, I was more surprised than anyone. Once again, Yesterday had been right. It seemed like everyone was interested in hearing about Coop and the things he had done to me. And the repeats were crazy. It was like almost all stations had picked up clips from the original interview.

One afternoon, I was on the bus heading home after a job interview. I paid, took my seat and was about to pull a novel out of my bag.

"'S'cuse me, but didn't I see you on TV last night?"

The older lady wasn't a person I'd strike up conversation with, but she'd asked me a question.

"Yes, ma'am, that was probably me."

"Umph." She had twisted up her mouth. "You never know what a man will do to a woman. My daughters and granddaughters love that man's music, but I told them, it was something about those eyes."

"Well, nobody is perfect," I'd said.

A wrinkled finger had shot up to quiet me. "No, don't make excuses for him. Men like that; they don't deserve an ounce of success. I don't care where they came from or how hard they worked. You can't mistreat people, then expect them to go quietly."

Everything she'd said was correct, but what good was it to complain to a complete stranger?

"Men like him, they don't deserve nothing good in life!"

She'd said it was such conviction, I knew without asking that she'd probably been with some just as bad in her day. She'd clearly spoken from experience.

"I'm glad you told your story. Think how many other women going through the same thing."

"Yeah, that wasn't how I looked at it, but I guess you have a good point there."

"Of course I do." She had leaned in, and I'd caught a whiff of an old fragrance my grandmother used to wear. "Look at you, you've bounced back. They see you happy. Now that you've moved on with your life, it gives them inspiration to do the same."

She'd patted my thigh.

If only she'd known.

"Ya did the right thing; big star or not, ya can't let no man treat you any ol' kind of way. If you do, they do what they want, how, and when, and you left stuck trying to pull everything back together."

When the bus had pulled up at my stop, I had popped up from the chair like burned toast running from the heat. She was putting me in a state of mind I wasn't ready to be in.

"Nice talking to you; this is where I get off," I'd said.

She had looked around like she wasn't sure whether it was her stop too.

"Oh, okay, well, you have a blessed day, ya hear me?"

I had gotten off the bus and made the nearly one-block trek to my apartment. The woman's words had rolled around in my head for a while, but I'd told myself it didn't matter what other people thought. She didn't know me, and if she'd gotten the impression that my life was together because I had left a selfish, abusive man, then maybe others who watched the interview would think the same.

As I'd dug for my key, at the front door, I'd told myself that it would be my turning point. I'd do a few more interviews, save the money, and try to get a lawyer who could help me get joint custody of my son.

It was dark when I'd pushed my door open and wondered how much time I had before I needed to get ready for my part-time job.

I'd felt around on the wall next to the door and flipped the switch on. My purse and the small bag I'd carried dropped to the floor at the sight of him.

"How the hell did you get in here?"

My eyes had searched the room for something I could grab and use to defend myself. He had no right to be in my apartment. If I was supposed to stay away from them, quite surely, they needed to stay away from me.

The emotions that had started to flare up in me were hard to ignore. My eyes instantly had started to swell with tears; I was so angry I wanted to kill him with my bare hands.

"You finally happy? Is this what you wanted?" His words weren't as sharp and crisp and his arms had flared. "My label is talking about delaying the release of my next single. We are going to lose lots of money over this."

His usually mesmerizing eyes had looked dull and glassy; he was broken. He would never actually say so, but the sound of his voice alone had told off on him. I'd felt an incredible sense of accomplishment, and I was nowhere near being done.

Could I have ruined his career, probably not, but if I could have caused him and my sister some misery, I would've been happy with that.

"You don't get it, do you?" he'd asked.

My tears had dried suddenly. There was so much I wanted to say to him, but I couldn't make the words sound right. I couldn't figure out how to hurt him half as much as he had hurt me.

"Get what, and where's Evelyn?"

His eyes had danced around the room, and suddenly, it had looked like he wasn't sure what to focus on.

"She had to go to L.A. to try and iron out a few things," he had admitted, with great reluctance.

"That bad, huh?"

I was celebrating on the inside at the sound of that news. I'd hoped it would take her a lifetime to clean things up. I couldn't wait for the next interview to air, and I was excited about doing even more. I'd talk to his high school paper, if they'd have me.

"We wasn't right for each other. You tried, you worked your ass off to try and help me get to where I am, but in the end, you just couldn't do it."

Talking sense wasn't Cooper's thing. He must've had lots of time to think about what he was going to say to me. I'd understood what he was trying to say, but I'd also understood that he probably didn't know how to piece the words together right.

I had done so much for *us*, but at the time, I thought I was working as much for my future as I was for his. It never dawned on me that he only saw me as a step toward his ultimate goal, and given the opportunity, he would take everything and leave me alone and with nothing.

"Evelyn was the real deal. She made the business side of it do what I couldn't, but Coop, I tried to warn you. I told you she wouldn't rest until she had *you*."

"So that's it, you still love me?"

His question had touched me to the core. It wasn't that I still loved him; I didn't. He had taught me enough to know, if he was able to treat me the way he did, it was clear Cooper only loved himself. But it was his arrogance that was hard for me to swallow.

"Still love you?" I had balked.

Cooper's expression had twisted ever so slightly. I couldn't determine whether he was surprised by my admission, or hurt that I wasn't still carrying a torch for his simple behind. The only thing he could do for me, was pay some of what was rightfully mine. Anything else was of little interest to me.

"Get real, Coop. You have taken extreme pleasure in stripping my life down to nothing and making me suffer. It was about time that I started to tell my side of the story. I did a lot for you. I did some shit—I'll never be able to say out loud, some shit that still keeps me up at night—and your funky ass is living life to the fullest."

He had hung his head low and taken his face into the palms of his hands. He had sighed hard and loud. But it wasn't until his leg had moved that I'd seen the tall, half-empty bottle.

Cooper had stood and looked down at me. "Where's the bathroom?"

He must've already been drunk. There were only two doors in my apartment, and he had already walked through one.

Despite what should've been obvious, I had pointed to my right, and he'd stumbled toward the door.

Alone with my thoughts, my mind had gone back to more memories of the pain he had caused.

Chapter Thirty-Six

Regardless of how badly I wanted and needed to go to L.A. with Cooper and Evelyn, we couldn't afford it. She or Sony paid for his ticket, but they weren't budgeted for mine. Every extra dollar we had went toward bills, so I had to stay back and watch my husband go on a business trip with the woman who was determined to ruin my marriage.

The thought that money was so crucial for us made me want to start looking for a regular job. In addition to not being able to move around like I needed, there were times late at night when I lay next to a snoring Coop, all I could do was think about how we'd eat the next day.

"So, are you just gonna keep blowing me up, even though you know I'm here on business?"

That was how Cooper finally answered the phone when I called for the umpteenth time. They had landed more than three hours prior to my call, and he didn't have the decency to let me know the plane didn't hit a mountain or anything like that.

"Well, hello to you too, husband!"

"Licia, why you trippin'? You know I'm working."

I heard Evelyn in the background, and I wanted to choke the shit out of her for being so close to him.

"Coop, you really need to relax before our meetings. I told you to turn the ringer off."

Could she be any more thirsty? Why would he need to turn his ringer off to relax before meeting his new colleagues? Evelyn was full of shit and she knew it. But she also knew my husband was talking to me on the phone and that her little comment would keep me up all night.

"Yeah, good point," Cooper said to her. I was sick because it was clear he no longer had a single independent thought of his own. If Eve didn't say it, it must not have been so, and I was sick of it.

They had flown out at six in the morning. They were in L.A. with time to spare by noon.

"Where are you guys stating?" I asked. I figured I could act as though I didn't hear Evelyn as she tried to coax him off the phone.

"We're at the Beverly Hills Hotel," Coop said. But the way he said it was almost like he was bragging. He kept up the drama between Evelyn and me. Anytime she did the smallest thing for him, he behaved as if it were earth-shattering. But when I worked my ass off for him, nothing was ever good enough.

"Coop, we really need to go over these notes, then I want you to take a nap," Evelyn said.

Again, her voice came across so loud, if I didn't know any better, I would've thought they were in the same bed and not about to have a conversation, either.

"Look, Licia, let me go. I need to rest before out meeting later tonight."

"Later tonight? What kind of meeting is this that happens at night?"

Cooper blew out a breath that was meant for me to hear.

"It's industry stuff, Licia. They don't conduct business out here during banker hours; nine to five is for the working poor out here," he said.

When I heard Eve laugh, it made me real desperate to commit murder. It was like she wanted me to hear her in the background. She knew I couldn't make the trip. But that was okay because I had something for both their asses.

"Coop, the masseuse is here," I heard Eve say, of course loud enough for me to hear. They needed a masseuse? What for and how was that a part of business?

"Look, I need to go, so I could relax before tonight," he said.

The minute I hung up with him, my cell rang, and it was the call I had been waiting on.

"This is Felicia Spears," I answered. I struggled to contain my excitement.

"Yes, this is Veronica Jackson, with Quick Payday Loans. We're calling to let you know that your loan has been approved, and the money will be deposited into your account within five minutes."

"Great! Thank you for the call."

Payday loans were the worst, with their incredible interest rates, but I was desperate. Eve thought she had the upper hand because she thought I couldn't make it to L.A. I couldn't wait to show up at the Beverly Hills Hotel and witness the look on their faces.

The ticket was already on a seventy-two-hour hold, so I just needed to pay and get to the airport.

"Mom." I called my mother the second I finished packing. "I need to bring Trey over." I couldn't tell her over the phone, but I needed to make sure she'd be available to watch him. "Something came up, and I needed to make sure he could stay there for a couple of days."

I picked up on the confusion in her voice, and I knew she had a million questions. But instead of allowing her to drill me, I talked fast and tried to convey the fact that I was in a hurry.

It didn't take long to get to her house, and like I knew she would be, she showed up in the doorway looking disheveled. She watched as I made my way into the house.

"What, where's the fire?" She wiped her hands on the apron she wore.

"I need to go to L.A.," I said.

My mother looked confused. She frowned a bit, then her head tilted ever so slightly.

"What you mean you going to L.A.? Like where Coop and Eve are?"

"Yes, that's the only L.A. I know," I snapped.

"Jesus be a fence!" my mother hollered, and her arms flared. I wasn't in the mood for any of her antics, and I was not about to be discouraged.

"I just need you to watch Trey. If my husband is meeting his team, as his wife, I need to be by his side. I should've flown out with them earlier."

Tabitha at a loss for words was not something that happened often. She stood in the doorway with an expression on her face that said she wasn't sure what she needed to do, but something was necessary.

"Well, chile, do they know you coming?" Her voice was laced with concern, and worry lines had invaded her face.

That's when I stopped cold in my tracks and whipped around to face her.

"Why would *they* need to be warned that I am coming? I am Cooper's wife. Truth be told, he should not have left without me in the first damn place."

My mother sighed, and retreated. She knew what I said was nothing but the gospel, and I dared her to challenge it, but she didn't get a chance.

When I heard the horn honking outside, I grabbed my bag and slid past my mother.

"My Uber ride is here. I'll call you once I land."

Chapter Thirty-Seven

The flight to L.A. was bumpy with lots of turbulence and a baby who cried during most of the flight. Despite all of this, I was more eager to land than anything. I couldn't wait to see the looks on Cooper's and Evelyn's faces when I showed up.

It didn't take long for the shit to hit the fan. I landed, hopped into another Uber and was taken directly to the Beverly Hills Hotel.

As I stormed into the lobby, it dawned on me that I never stopped to make a reservation or anything. I slowed down a bit and tried to think fast on my feet. How would I find them? And where would I stay?

"Ma'am, are you checking in?"

If that bellman hadn't asked that question, I may have had time to think clearly. But in front of all those people, I simply nodded and walked up to the registration desk. There was no turning back, so I decided to take my chances.

"Hi, I'm Felicia Spears, and my husband left a key for me," I said with all confidence, as I stepped up to the clerk who asked if she could help. Of course, he had done no such thing, but I was hoping I could catch someone off their game.

The clerk was young, cheerful, and seemed eager to please.

"Okay," she said, and started typing. She grinned hard and wide as her eyes focused in on her computer screen. "Let me see here."

Perspiration began to drizzle down the middle of my back.

The smile seemed to melt from her face, quickly replaced by a frown. "Uh, I don't see any notes," she stammered as she studied the computer screen.

"It's okay. I just need a key to my husband's room."

She gave me a blank stare, then looked down at her screen again. Suddenly, her face turned red and she stammered. She glanced around as if she were looking for help. When I didn't see anyone rushing to her aid, I got firm.

"Look, I'm tired, I've been on an hours-long flight, and I want to get into my room and relax. I need a key to the room, so I can go up."

"Ma'am, uh, I don't see any notes on Mr. Spears' account."

"I didn't ask what you see. I'm telling you I need a key to the room." I pulled my wallet and snatched my Texas driver's license out, and smacked it onto the counter.

"Do you see what this says?" I pointed at my name beneath the photo.

The clerk looked down at it, then around again. She cleared her throat and focused back on the computer screen.

"Ma'am. I cannot give you a key to a room unless a note is left for you that specifies that."

"Where is your manager?" I asked. I got a little loud. I was wrong, but it wasn't like I had a plan.

"Ma'am, I've already reached out to him. I think he's out to lunch. I just need you to calm down."

"Calm down? Don't tell me to calm down! My husband is here for an important meeting, and he needs my support, and you're here acting like it's a crime to give his wife access to his room."

The line behind me was growing. Suddenly, another desk clerk walked up.

"Lacy, is everything okay?" He didn't look friendly, and I figured it was time for me to give up and think of another plan.

"You know what, it's okay; I'll call his cell and tell him to call you guys."

Before she could explain everything to her coworker, I stepped aside and watched as they struggled to help other people in the line. It pissed me off that I couldn't bully Lacy into giving up the key or even the room number.

As I walked to another part of the lobby, I noticed a sign that advertised the hotel's spa services. Instantly, I had a plan.

Once I made my way up to the floor that housed the spa, I passed by the office, put my bag into the stairwell, and stormed back to the office's smoky glass doors. I pulled the door open, listened to the peaceful chime, and broke the silence of the atmosphere.

"I need to talk to somebody who's in charge," I yelled.

One woman's eyes grew wide with fear, and the other who stood next to her looked just as concerned.

"Ma'am, can you lower your voice, please?" one of the women asked.

"Who did the massages for my husband yesterday evening? Whatever oil you guys used has caused a major allergic reaction. That cheap shit got on our sheets, he's all welted up, and now I think I'm about to have a reaction myself."

"Ma'am, let me check and see what's going on," the woman, who was standing as I walked in, said. "Look up the records from yesterday," she instructed the seated woman.

The woman moved closer to me, but when the brunette rattled off a name and room number, I had everything I needed.

"Cicely is one of our most experienced masseuses. I can't imagine her using anything that might create that type of reaction. Where's your husband now?" She spoke to me in a tone that said she was really concerned.

"You know what, now that I'm thinking about it, you're right. His friend rushed him to an emergency room, but I have a feeling I know exactly what happened. I'm sorry; I was just so crazy thinking about what happened to his skin."

"Here, let me get you some water. Are you experiencing any difficulties?"

"No, but I couldn't be sure. I just wanted to come and talk with you guys to see if we could figure something out."

"Well, the fact that you didn't have any problems leaves me encouraged. We use the same oils during our couple's massage. Can you call and check up on your husband?"

I started getting flustered. Now that I had the room number, I didn't want them to make any calls or try to verify my story. I now knew that Evelyn had booked a couple's massage; what kind of business trip requires a couple's anything?

"Yes, I'm going to call him, but I'm just glad to know it wasn't anything you guys did. Let me go back up to the room, and as soon as I hear from him, I'll call and let you guys know what's going on."

"Okay," the woman said.

She walked over to the desk and looked over the woman's shoulder. "Missus Spears, we will be waiting to hear back from you."

"Okay," I said as I walked out of their office.

Once I made my way up to the floor, I saw a cleaning cart between the two rooms but couldn't tell which one was being cleaned. It was just my luck it was the room next door being cleaned.

It was late morning, and I hoped the couple would be out. The moment I saw the lady knock at the door and wait, I kept an eye on her.

At first, I thought my luck had finally run its course—until she pulled her key out and opened the room door. I waited for ten minutes, then I rushed down the hall.

"Ah, no need to clean," I said as I rushed into the room. She was in the bathroom.

I kicked off my shoes, tossed my bag in the corner, and grabbed the ice bucket. The little woman walked out of the bathroom and looked at me over her glasses.

"You don't want housekeeping?"

"No. I had an awful headache, so I went to grab some ice. I meant to put the sign on the door, but I guess I forgot. You were working on the room next door, so I thought I'd be able to catch you before you started."

She looked confused, then I saw her eyes drop to a chart that hung from the side of her cleaning cart. "Says here, to clean."

"It's okay." I grabbed a twenty-dollar bill and slid it to her. She looked at me oddly, but made her way out of the room. Once she was gone, I closed the door and decided to start my wait.

I wasn't sure how long they'd been gone or when they'd return, but like Cooper had told me, they didn't do business during the day, so I figured they were out getting food, or sightseeing.

There was one king-sized bed, which was definitely reason for concern. There were champagne flutes with two empty bottles, and a plate had what was left of the strawberries. Three scented candles were in the room, and that made it clear that the evening was about a whole lot more than business.

In the closet, dresses and blouses hung among the men's blazers, slacks, and neckties. I swallowed back tears. All of the evidence told me that Evelyn and Cooper were quite comfortable in the affair that was going on.

Chapter Thirty-Eight

N early two hours had passed since I'd made my way into the hotel room, and I was still alone. My mind raced with thoughts about what the two had been doing their first night in Los Angeles together. For all I knew, there was probably never a business meeting. More than likely, Evelyn had created the entire cover about the meeting, so she could come and screw my husband.

I had been walking around the room inspecting everything from the paperwork to the toiletries. It was very clear that the couple was exactly that, a couple. In her toiletries bag, she had massage oils, several sex toys, and nipple clips. Who needs those items on a business trip?

"Fucking home-wrecking bitch!"

My eyes were tired of the tears, and I went in and out of rage as I found something else that indicated my sister was sleeping with my husband. She had slutty lingerie and fur-covered house slippers. The bitch knew what she was coming here to do.

"They probably fucked all day, eating strawberries, and drinking champagne, then got dressed up and went out at night looking like the perfect little couple."

Suddenly, an idea popped into my head. I took out the very expensive-looking iron and turned it on. I pulled out the ironing board and turned the iron up as high as it would go. I removed all Evelyn's dresses, laid them on the board one by one, and placed the iron down on it. Why should that bitch be able to walk around dressed up and holding on to my husband like he is hers?

It took seconds for the fabric to melt beneath the hot iron. By the time I got to the third dress, the room started to smell of smoke and burned plastic, so I walked over and lowered the temperature to sixty degrees.

On some pieces I burned two spots to make sure there was no way anything could be salvaged. It took less than thirty minutes to brand each piece of hers and Cooper's clothing with a large black iron spot.

"That should teach their asses," I said as I stood back and looked over my work. If there was more I could have done, I would have. I just wanted the two of them to come back.

"Maybe I should trash the room?" I looked around and tried to think about the most damage I could do.

I unplugged the iron and put everything back into the closet. While I wanted to see the look on their faces when they discovered what I had done, I knew that wasn't possible, but it gave me pleasure when I conjured up in my mind the ways in which I knew Evelyn would be pissed.

It didn't take long for someone to come fumbling at the door. I got excited as I heard them. I didn't know whether I should sit on the bed, go hide in the closet, or open the door to let them in.

There was so much giggling and sweet-talking going on, I wondered whether they would actually come into the room.

But a little while later, the door swung open, and Evelyn stepped in loaded down with shopping bags. She dropped them at the sight of me. By the time Cooper whipped around, he nearly bumped into her.

"What the fuck are you doing here?" Evelyn spat. Her eyes quickly darted around the room. "How the hell did you get in here?"

I never said a word to her. My eyes stayed glued to my husband.

I quietly searched his expression for any signs of guilt or even remorse, but there was none.

Evelyn turned to him. "I thought you were gonna do it this afternoon."

"Yeah, it's being done, or was supposed to be," Cooper said.

As I watched them whisper to each other, I wondered how long it would take for Cooper to say something to me.

"If I took out a gun and fucking killed you both right now, do you think I could get away with it?" The sinister laugh I released wasn't planned, but it was a nice added touch.

Instantly, Evelyn's eyes grew wide. "Whoa, that's a threat!" she said as she backed up and moved closer to Cooper. "You think she has a gun?"

I stepped up. "You don't know what I have," I said and mimicked like I was about to swing on her. Evelyn flinched and moved completely behind my husband.

"See, if you had done it before we left like I told you, she wouldn't have followed us all the way across the country to act like some lovesick puppy."

"What is *it*? What the hell should he have done, Evelyn? Go ahead, tell me; what is *it* that you told him to do?"

"Serve your ass with divorce papers," she snapped from behind Cooper's back.

Sure, I had come to L.A., swindled my way into the hotel room, and found hard evidence that my husband and my sister were having an affair. But hearing her say that Cooper was serving me with divorce papers, literally made me snap.

Before I could think about it, I grabbed a tall lamp and hurled it across the room at them. Cooper ducked and it sideswiped Evelyn. She screamed, opened the hotel room door, and took off running down the hall and screaming for security.

Knowing I didn't have much time, I snatched the clock and several other items I could move, and plummeted Cooper with them all.

"You stinking low-life bastard!" I screamed as I swung on him.

He cowered toward a corner and used his arms to try and protect his face.

I spat on him, and kicked him as hard as I could in the ribs before I rushed out of the room. Once outside, I looked up and down the halls in both directions. When I didn't see Evelyn, I ran into the stairwell where I had left my bag. Instead of going back into the hall, I took the stairs up a few floors in hopes of giving myself some time to get away.

That was how my lousy marriage ended, in a hotel room on the other side of the country where I'd followed my husband and his mistress to confront them about my suspicion. But obviously, I had been too late.

Chapter Thirty-Nine

Three hours later, the truth serum that was in the bottle of vodka near Cooper's leg was nearly gone. It started when I watched him pick up the bottle, take it to his lips, and pull in a long swig.

I watched with interest as his Adam's apple danced when the liquid flowed down his throat.

There was no point in being mad about him being inside my place, because he looked like he was comfortable. I figured he either flashed a smile or came up with something fabulous like an autograph for my landlord. There was no damage to the door or any of the windows, so I knew it wasn't a break-in.

Before Cooper put the bottle back down, he extended it in my direction and nodded slightly.

I hesitated, but declined.

Cooper shrugged.

Before he gestured to take the bottle back to his lips, I grabbed his arm and stopped him. I held the bottle for a second before I pulled it to my lips. The liquid burned the moment it touched my tongue and felt like fire as it slid down my throat. But it was good.

"Aeey, don't be greedy," Cooper said, as he jokingly grabbed the bottle from me. He took another swig, then passed it back to me.

We did this in silence for a while, until my throat wouldn't accept any more. After the initial burn from my first few sips, I felt good. I didn't feel as good as I would have if I had one of my cocktails, but I felt good.

When Cooper tried to pass me the bottle again, I gestured with my hand to let him know I couldn't handle another taste. My head felt light, and I was scared I might lose control over my ability to keep it all together. There was no way in hell I wanted to break down in front of him.

After a bit more silence, my mouth seemed to take over. "You really fucked everything up with us." I felt the unsteady words as they wobbled from my lips, but I had no power to stop myself. He had messed it all up.

But most of it was my fault for being so dumb and blind. All of the signs were there as far as Cooper was concerned. He wasn't even smart enough to try and cover his selfishness. He put it out there and gave me the option to deal with it, if I wanted. It seemed the more I accepted, the more bullshit and antics he pushed.

I had lived in a car with Cooper when we were homeless. We had been in the struggle together. We stayed with my mother longer than we should have because he'd blow most of his paycheck on fancy clothes and shoes. His excuse was always the same: "The good stuff don't go on sale, and I need to look the part 'cause I'm gonna be a star one day."

Again, I was the fool because I'd bite my tongue and found a way to clean up the financial messes he created.

"I wasn't trying to, but I could see the big picture, and I felt like it was hard for you to see my vision."

Could he be any more stupid? Everything I did, was for the vision, *our* vision, or what I thought was ours, but he knew all along was his own.

"See your vision? I worked to help create the vision, then adjusted it so you could see and appreciate it."

I felt some kind of way about him thinking he was the one who had orchestrated the plan we'd still be on had he not veered off course.

"The way you talking, sounds like you think I only got a taste for the good life because you hipped me to it." Sarcasm dripped from his words. I watched as he took another drink.

"I was born to be a star, destined from birth. It just wasn't happening as fast as I wanted. I knew from the day I stepped out my mama's womb that I had that fiyah, but when it didn't happen the way I wanted, I took a few detours."

Cooper extended his arms and leaned back onto my bed. "Everybody knew I'd make it one day; that was never a question. The only thing that was uncertain was the path I'd take."

"Is that what we were to you, a detour?"

He sat up. "Licia, I didn't dream of being a husband and a father when I was a kid. I dreamed about being on stage, filling stadiums and thrilling crowds. Just like little girls want to be brides, I wanted to be a star."

He had me fooled. For years while we were together, I thought Cooper was content in his roles as husband, father, and employee. If I had known we were just weights that kept him anchored, maybe I would not have agreed to manage his career.

"Don't get me wrong; I don't regret my son. Shiiiid, my legacy is solidified with that lil' mofo, but if I had to do it again, I would have moved around differently."

To me, that translated into he would not have married me. Again, even under the influence, Coop didn't have enough common sense needed to filter his words.

I was pissed.

"So you don't regret our son, but you regret *us*," I said.

"We should have never mixed the two, that's all."

What the hell was that supposed to mean? Fury began to brew in the pit of my stomach. I grabbed the bottle in hopes that another swallow could help suppress the mounting rage.

"You could've been my manager early on, but on a team," he said. "I think you bit off more than any one person could chew."

Cooper chuckled a bit as if he savored a private joke.

"Hell, I know I'ma handful."

The way he spoke was as if I should've been happy with the consolation prize he had graciously offered. After all I had done for him, he could still sit back and point out areas where I was ineffective.

"The difference between you and Evelyn," he pointed to the side of his head, "She's gonna use her smarts. That woman knows what she's doing, and she's gonna get the job done at any cost."

My eyes narrowed.

Was he serious? Could he have been that stupid all along? How had this turned into yet another opportunity to sing Evelyn's praises?

"You're really clueless, huh?"

Although I said the words, and I laughed at the thought, on the inside, I was pissed by his ignorance and his constant need to bring up Evelyn.

The taunting was too much.

"Whaaat? All I'm saying is where you was giving it up out both sides of the panties, Evelyn would never get down like that."

I froze at his statement.

Words escaped me; I had no idea he knew. Imagine I'd done and given everything in an attempt to help *his* career, and still he'd left me the moment he thought a better opportunity had come along.

"So all I did for you didn't mean a thing?"

I walked away from him and toward my closet. I stooped down and pulled in a breath. I tried to shake crazy thoughts from my head, but he wouldn't shut up. It didn't matter that he knew the extent of all I had done for him; now it was clear he didn't even give a damn.

"I mean, I ain't saying it didn't mean anything, but I also wasn't trying to be fucked up over it, either." He shrugged. "Men not like women. Y'all can forgive us when we step out, but this the type of cat I am. Once I know you out there like that, I just chill back."

When a man knew his woman was sleeping with someone else, and he couldn't care less, that said a lot about the man. I was all messed up for what I had done, but I'd done it for him, thinking it eventually would have been for us.

Cooper shrugged. "Shiiid, I figured you was just trying to get your body count up."

My head whipped in his direction. Get my body count up? I was doing what I had to do to keep him busy and singing, and he thought I was trying to see how many men I could sleep with? Who does that?

"Shit, you grown, who am I to tell you what to do if you wanna give them the biz?"

Suddenly, it felt like I had floated above my body and watched my hand as it reached for and clutched one of the red-bottoms, the very ones he had bought for my mother.

Chapter Forty

Cooper sat on my bed, eased back like we were old friends who had just enjoyed each other's company. Sure, we were both feeling the effects of the liquor. His speech slurred a bit, and I felt weak on my legs.

But Cooper obviously felt safe in my presence, despite what he'd said the interviews had done to his career. I knew his wife, my sister, didn't know he was here with me; she would never tolerate that.

But here he was, relaxed, leaned back, and talking about how different his life was now than the early years with me. He was drunk and so was I. But under the influence was the only way we were able to fake being cordial. This man thought it was okay to tell me how my shortcomings had held him back over the years. He told me that my sister was a better match for him.

I may not have still been in love with Cooper, but his words were lethal, and they cut me to my core.

"I don't know where things took a turn with us," he had the nerve to say.

That comment made my head swim. I definitely had some ideas.

He didn't know where things took a turn with us? Was it when I was prostituting myself to jumpstart your career? Or maybe it was when I risked my own freedom and went to jail holding your weed. But if not that, maybe it was the many times I had to grovel and beg to get management at a venue to not fire you. Or better yet, all the times I warned you that my backstabbing sister was out to sabotage our marriage, but you went behind my back and fucked her anyway.

"People outgrow each other," I said. I put the shoe down. There was no way I should've entertained the thoughts that floated around in my head. But I could hardly resist. It would be so easy, fast, and best of all, it would be completely unexpected.

He was still the same ole self-centered, selfish, narcissistic Cooper he'd always been. Despite all the wrong he had done, he had come out of it all completely unscathed, even better than before.

The bad press he'd received may have pushed back the release of a song, but he'd bounce back, because he knew his fans would forgive and forget. He'd come out of it unscathed. And maybe one day, he'd have the balls to actually write about it in his next hit song.

I had no love for him after what he had done to me. I actually felt pure hatred. The fact that he behaved like we should be above all that went down burned my insides until I couldn't stand it anymore.

What if the judge knew *he* was here? Would he face jail for breaking his own restraining order? I knew he had very little to do with that order. I understood that came from my sister, but the fact that he allowed her to do it burned me up. When we were together, Cooper was the epitome of an alpha male. He did what he wanted, when and how, and he never made any apologies for it. But once he got under Evelyn's spell, it was like he never had another independent thought of his own.

Everything he said or did was based on something Evelyn said or suggested.

"Look, Licia, we need to quit all this craziness. You know like I do that people love drama. When you let your misplaced aggression get the best of you, and you start trashing me in the press, baby, it only makes you look bad." He shrugged easily.

My "misplaced aggression"?

He didn't notice the twitch of my right eye, because he had the floor and he'd never stop to consider anyone else's feelings during his time to shine. Absolutely nothing had changed about Cooper.

"Now, you got Evelyn running around here trying to contain all these fires, and she looking at me with a serious side-eye, you know it ain't a good look at all."

He was right; it wasn't a good look, but the fact that he thought he could come over with a bottle of liquor and talk some sense into me was baffling, if not insane. I was fresh off my most recent arrest where I'd spent weeks in jail because of him and his hateful wife, and he wanted to talk about what wasn't a good look?

"I ain't trying to go all-out like Eve, talking about defamation lawsuits and all that other bull. I'm like, we all grown and shit; I'ma just go and try to reason with her."

Now the real reason for his visit was starting to surface. I knew he had come with an agenda, but I couldn't be sure what it was.

"So, Evelyn wants to file a lawsuit against me? It ain't enough that I just spent weeks behind bars over some pettiness, but now she wants to sue me too?"

I flapped my arms around. "What y'all gon' take? I ain't got shit. You saw to that; you took everything and left me completely broke. What y'all gonna take now?"

My sudden outburst seemed to catch him off guard.

"I dunno why y'all hate each other like that. That shit ain't natural. I mean y'all came from the same womb and yet y'all act like nothing less than enemies. Even strangers treat each other better."

He always hated when I talked about Evelyn. It didn't matter how wrong she was or how stupid the moves she made, he never wanted me to talk about *her*.

"What does Evelyn say about all of this?"

Cooper made a smacking noise with his mouth as he pulled in air. He shook his head and confessed, "Well, she lost her lid when

I told her I wanted to talk to you, but you know me, Licia, I do what a man's gotta do. She mad, but she gon' be all right."

He turned to me. "But it's you I'm worried about."

Cooper's face even twisted into a pained expression.

I nearly laughed out loud at that comment and his expression, for real.

Cooper wasn't worried when he took a flight with his mistress across the country, had me served and tossed all of my shit outside of the apartment we shared. He wasn't worried when he cut off access to my one and only child, and he damn sure wasn't worried when he had me thrown in jail for violating a protective order just because I wanted to see my son. But there was no need for me to point any of that out. My mind was already made up.

He barely noticed when I grabbed the stiletto shoe again. I gripped it in the palm of my hand and released it. Then I gripped it again and clutched it tightly.

Before I could think about what I was doing, the horror in Cooper's eyes said he finally saw it coming, but it was too late. He was shocked as the spiked heel came barreling down and struck him in the side of his neck.

I swung as hard as I could. All of my weight went down and forced the heel to make contact with his skin.

Blood gushed from the area like a busted fire hydrant. His expression never changed as he tumbled onto his back, clutched toward his neck, and struggled to remove the shoe. It was lodged in past nearly half of the spiked five-inch heel.

"You have ruined my entire life. You took every damn thing from me, then you come back here and act like we're old friends shooting the shit."

He gasped for air and flapped around like a fish that had jumped out of its bowl.

"I fucking hate you!"

Blood was everywhere. It splattered on the walls, drenched my clothes and the sheets.

I couldn't move.

He needed to know the pain he'd caused me. I watched as life literally drained from his face. After a few minutes of him squirming and kicking on the floor, he suddenly stopped and the air in the room went completely still. His eyes were still open and seemed focused on me.

That's when I reached for the phone and dialed 9-1-1.

No one had to tell me when Cooper Spears died, because I witnessed it with my own eyes. It was wrong, but I felt like I had made that man what he was, and I had every right to take him out after all he had done to me.

"Nine-one-one, what is your emergency?" the dispatch operator said into my ear.

"Uh, yes, I need to report a death. Cooper Spears is dead," I said.

"Cooper Spears, as in the singer Cooper Spears?" The dispatch operator's voice took an obvious dip. She lost all professionalism.

Really? I couldn't believe that the dispatcher was trying to get clarification about *who* had actually died. I held the phone and stood quietly.

Yes, Cooper Spears finally got what was coming to him, and he deserved exactly what he got.

About The Author

By day, Pat Tucker works as a radio news director in Houston, Texas. By night, she is a talented writer with a knack for telling page-turning stories. A former TV news reporter, she draws on her background to craft stories readers will love. She is the author of ten novels and has participated in three anthologies, including *New York Times* bestselling author Zane's *Caramel Flava*. A graduate of San Jose State University, Pat is a member of the National and Houston Association of Black Journalists and Sigma Gamma Rho Sorority, Inc. She is married with two children.

If you enjoyed "All About Him," be sure to check out

GUARDING SECRETS

BY PAT TUCKER
AVAILABLE FROM STREBOR BOOKS

CHAPTER ONE
KENYA TAYE

I always said I'd rather slice my own wrists with a butter knife than give head. Yet here I was. On my knees, I struggled to stay focused. It was hard because my knees throbbed and my jaws hurt. But that ache was nothing compared to the intense pain I felt in my heart. Still I worked.

I wanted him to feel good.

When he finally exploded, I exhaled, and fell back onto my butt. I used the back of my hand to wipe my mouth.

"Daaaymn, ma! That was good. You the best, ma." He groaned, and sounded spent.

For a long time afterward, all you could hear was us breathing loudly and heavily in the small, dark, area. That was the only sound until I mustered up the courage to say what I had practiced in my mind.

It wasn't easy for me because I loved DaQuan Cooper like I loved my right arm. But DaQuan only loved himself—and money.

"You know what, DaQuan; you a good-for-nothing liar and a low-down cheat, a straight-cold heartbreaker." My chest tightened, but I sucked in some air, drew my eyebrows together and blurted out the rest of the words I'd been dying to say. "I don't even understand why I let you do the things you do to me."

When I glanced up into his shifty eyes, he didn't seem the least bit pressed by my words. He looked like he was still lost in bliss, but his pleasure was just that, his alone. He didn't give a damn about whether or not I was satisfied.

A few tears gushed from my eyes and I felt even worse. I quickly wiped them away. I cringed inside and wanted to crumble right there on the floor. He had gotten his, was completely satisfied, but I still felt empty.

"Aww, c'mon, ma; you don't mean none of that."

He touched my chin and lifted my head. Those intense eyes locked onto mine and I felt completely trapped, stuck like I was attached with super-strength Krazy Glue. I stared into his eyes.

Was there a slight trace of something in those eyes? I wanted desperately to see some love there, but deep down, I knew there wasn't.

My brain was confused; even though I was mad, the way he looked at me still made me feel warm all over. There was something intense and electrifying about our connection. The thrill of it all made my stomach churn.

His cool and calm demeanor was just the right amount of swagger that drove me bananas. All of a sudden, my anger seemed like it was about to melt. Now, all those things I'd said, felt stupid and pointless.

He was everything! In all my twenty-eight years, I ain't never loved a man the way I loved DaQuan.

I shook the traitorous thoughts from my head.

Stay focused! I silently coached myself.

Enough was enough! It wasn't gonna work this time. His intense eyes that pulled me in, his touch that made me happy. I was sick and tired of him and his bullshit. I'd risked everything for him. Everything, and he couldn't care less.

"My family and friends all tell me I should leave you alone. This thing has gone way too far." My voice was shakier than I wanted, but those words had to be said.

He didn't say nothing. Instead, he swung his leg over my head and got up from the makeshift bed. He grabbed an old rag, wiped at his crotch, then tugged on one side of his underwear and pant leg. He balanced himself on one foot, stepped into his clothes and pulled them up.

DaQuan moved away from me, but his essence was still on the tip of my tongue.

The air in the room was thick. It was a mixture of sex, tension, and cleaning products. But it was like I was the only one who noticed or even cared.

"I 'ont know why you let them thirsty bitches get in yo head like that. They 'ont know nothing about us and how we carry it, ma."

He had turned his broad back to me, and I was annoyed.

"DaQuan—"

He adjusted his clothes and moved toward the door, like he didn't hear me call his name. I sat frozen, on the floor, unable to move. I needed a moment to get my shit together.

There was no way I could go back out there with nothing solid from him. I needed to hear him tell me he loved me. I had practiced those words for weeks. I thought about if they were too strong, or if they'd be enough to get a response, but I never considered there would be nothing.

I expected so much more from him.

Suddenly, tears poured from my eyes like a busted faucet. It was like I had lost all ability to control my emotions. And he still couldn't care less; he didn't give a damn. The bottom line was, to him, I was just another one of his workers, plain and simple. He walked out of the closet and left me alone with my tears.

Hours later, I sat inside the guards' booth and thought about ways to get things back on point with me and DaQuan. My mood was foul because he wouldn't act the way I wanted him to act. There was no doubt that he ran the place and could do whatever he wanted, but I needed him to make it clear that I was his number one. Damn the rest of 'em. In a prison, possession was everything.

My mind was so deep in thought, I nearly missed Edwards and Bishop when they bounced into the booth.

"Hey, what's wrong?" Correctional Officer Diane Edwards asked.

We all wore the standard issue uniform; black pants, white shirts, with a belt and steel-toed boots. But Edwards always flipped her collar. She starched it so that it would stand up all day.

She had a gum-bearing smile that was too big for her small face. Despite her slim and lanky frame, as a correctional officer, she had no problems with respect from the inmates.

Quiet Jane Bishop, on the other hand, was thick and considered mean unless she liked you. The three of us rounded out DaQuan's A-team, with two other officers, Richard Swanson and Billy Franklin. The females held it down during the day and the guys acted as our backup. He had another crew that worked the night shift.

"Nothing. I'm cool. Just been feeling kinda sick lately," I said.

"Oh?" Edwards' eyebrows went up.

I playfully swatted in her direction as if to knock what she implied into a lie.

"Don't start that mess, with me, D," I said.

She pursed her lips and raised both eyebrows.

"Whaaaat? I ain't sayin' nothing!" Edwards said.

Bishop stepped closer. "Hey, let's go check out the newbies. They're wrapping up their last session before they get their assignments."

I swirled my chair around. "Do we get anybody this go-round?"

"Yeah, I think so. I wanna say two," Bishop said.

"Let's go mean-mug 'em real quick," Edwards said. "It'll help you feel better."

DaQuan had left me in a sour mood, but the last thing I wanted to do was alert my girls to trouble between us, so I shook it off. Maybe checking out our new underlings would help me feel better. If nothing else, it would take my mind away from my complicated situation with DaQuan.

"Where they at? And who's teaching the class?" I asked.

"C.O. Owens got it this time. C'mon, let's roll," Edwards said.

I followed them to the part of the building with the classrooms, and we slid inside just as the group was getting up for a fifteen-minute break.

"I need some water; let's go into the break room."

Edwards and Bishop followed me into the break room where a few of the new hires hung out.

New correctional officers always brought new and interesting twists to the job. I hoped we'd get some team players this time around.

CHAPTER TWO
CHARISMA JONES

"Cha-ris-mah? Umph, where'd you get a name like that?"

The question broke my concentrated train of thought and pulled my focus away from the dreary gray walls inside the windowless room. The room smelled dank like mold had grown somewhere close by, and the constant hum from the appliances irritated me. My eyes quickly grazed over the woman who had asked. I didn't try to hide my irritation.

It was a common question, so I was used to people asking. Still, I allowed my cold gaze to travel up her thin body, stopped at her name tag that read *Bishop*, and continued up to her handsome face.

Why was she so perplexed by my God-given name in the first place? Why couldn't people ever mind their own damn business?

I wasn't trying to make new friends. My circle was small for a reason and I wasn't about to change that just because I was new to the job.

"My daddy named me after this chick he loved."

"Oh, yo mama?" she asked.

"No. His chick on the side."

Bishop's eyes grew wide, and her mouth fell open.

I gulped down the remainder of my water from the paper cup, crumbled the cup, and tossed it into the wastepaper basket. I shrugged, then turned to leave. Her expression was still frozen with her mouth agape.

By the time I'd made my way back to my seat, I was more than ready for the break to be over. This was not a social gathering and I wasn't under the false impression that it was. I was there because I desperately needed the job, and that was the best I could do for the time being.

From the corner of my eye, I saw Bishop and another correctional officer as they strolled by, whispered to each other, and another woman. They all turned and looked at me.

I rolled my eyes as I fell onto the chair and hoped the fifteen-minute break was the last for the day. I was in the final part of a mandatory training class for my new position at the Texas Department of Criminal Justice's Jester Unit, a prison of about 300 inmates, and I was already tired of what I was certain would be an uninspiring, dead-end job.

But what choice did I have? It was all I could get and I'd been lucky to get it.

A hot wave of humiliation washed over me every time I thought about the fact that I even had to accept this position.

We needed to wrap up training and get on with the job. This is not what my life was supposed to be. I had actually gone to college, for Christ's sake! When the instructor finally moved to the front of the room, I was relieved. We needed to wrap this up.

Sweat made his white uniform shirt look more like the color pink as it stuck to his skin. Every few seconds, he swiped his hand through his greasy, dirty-blond hair and sweat ran down the sides of his head. C.O. Owens looked down at a piece of paper on his desk, then began.

"This is the start of your career in law enforcement. You are not here to make friends; you are here to help keep an eye on people who could not obey the law. They are the bad guys."

Beefy fingers went through his hair again.

"There's a very thin line between being the guard and the animals being guarded. If you break the law, you will be brought up on charges, and you will turn into the animals being guarded."

Owens walked to the edge of his desk, pivoted, then walked back again. I could've sworn some sweat went airborne when he turned. But that might have been my imagination because I was bored. I adjusted myself in the chair and struggled to focus.

"Please, if you forget everything else I tell you, do not forget you are not here to make friends. This is the jungle."

The more he moved and talked, the more sweat poured from his hairline and down over his face.

"In here, it is a them against us mentality. You already know, misery ain't happy unless it's got some company, and these inmates will try each and every day to drag you down with them. They're lonely and they want company."

He paused, exhaled and looked around the room, then asked, "Does anyone have any questions?" He stopped at the desk again, looked at a notepad, then back out at the group. When no one raised a hand, he looked back at his paper and continued.

I sighed hard.

"You are not here to socialize or fraternize with inmates. If you're looking for a date, this ain't the place. You want to mingle with these guys, or hook up these guys, or go into business with these guys, get ready to go to jail. It is illegal for you to carry on a relationship, any kind of relationship, with an inmate confined to the Texas Department of Criminal Justice."

Once again, he paused like we needed time to digest what he'd said.

"You've been warned. Especially you women," he said, then snickered. He pulled at his uniform shirt. "This uniform is a target; they will be out to get you. You will hear endless sob stories. They will compliment you, flirt with you. They will say, and do, whatever they can to get you to break the rules because their lives are miserable, and they have nothing but time on their hands."

He walked again.

"If he's so handsome, and so incredibly irresistible, and you must have him because your pathetic lives just don't lead you to anyone in the free world, wait until the sorry bastard is done serving his sentence!"

He snapped his fingers. Once again, he looked around, then asked, "Do any of you have any questions?"

When no one said a word, he looked down at his paper again. "Well, since none of you have questions, you know the rules. You've been warned. There are a couple of lists near the door. Check them for your name and number; that's gonna tell you your assigned department. Some of y'all already met some of your new coworkers. Be on time, learn the ropes, follow the chain of command, do what you're supposed to do, and you'll be fine."

He looked around the room again. "Welcome to the Texas Department of Criminal Justice."

That day, I had no clue that his warning would one day haunt me during my time at TDCJ.